/英·檢·保·證·班/

全民英檢 初級 保證班

閱讀與寫作

三大特色
- 完全配合英檢試題
- 掌握英語學習要領
- 模擬試題，實戰演練

　英檢過關 Easy Go！

初碧華/著

書泉出版社 印行

目 錄
Contents

閱讀能力測驗
Part I Reading Test

閱讀技巧 2
Chapter 1 Reading Skills

文法要點 6
Chapter 2 Grammar Points

模擬測驗及解答 132
Chapter 3 Mock Test & Answer

寫作能力測驗

閱讀能力測驗

Part I
Reading Test

第一章 閱讀技巧

（1）須熟悉作答說明及範例

第一部分：詞彙和結構

本部分共 **15** 題，每題含一個空格。請就試題冊上 **A、B、C、D** 四個選項中選出最適合題意的字或詞，標示在答案紙上。

1. **Our teacher always asks us to _____ lessons before coming to class.**
   A. decide
   B. review
   C. preview
   D. receive

   正確答案為（**C**），請在答案紙上塗黑作答。

【說明】

此題或許有同學會認為 B. review（複習）也是正確的答案，因為老師會要求學生上課前要先複習功課，但是就題意來說，上課前一般老師會要求學生先預習要上的部分，以便能充分吸收老師授課的內容，而下課前會叮嚀學生回家要複習所上的內容，以便能儲存更久，進一步轉化成自己的知識。另外，若題目改成：Our teacher always asks us to _____ the **old** lessons before coming to class. 或 Our teacher always asks us to _____ the old lessons after class. 則答案便只能選 B. review（複習）了。

（2）瞭解自己在閱讀方面的弱點，然後再加以改進。

　　例如：若字彙過少，則加強單字的吸收。若閱讀缺乏耐心，則可嘗試從簡易有趣的文章著手，即使兒童讀物也無妨。等到發展出一些基礎，培養出對英語的喜好和耐心後，再去挑戰難度較高的文章。

（3）拿到文章先作瀏覽，以掌握文章的大意。若平常閱讀，則瀏覽過後，須從頭細讀，邊做筆記、附註，閱讀完後，仍應試著回想所讀之內容。

（4）不要逐字閱讀，尤其在應考時，以免影響閱讀速度，進而妨礙對內容的理解。應儘量培養閱讀字群的習慣。

（5）不要太專注於細節，而忽略了更重要的文章主旨。亦即勿「見樹不見林」。

（6）平時閱讀，即應養成勤查字典的習慣，但切勿一見到生字就查字典，以免養成依賴字典的習慣，同時避免拖延閱讀速度。此外，查字典最好針對生字的用法及例句做了解，而不是光查該單字的意思而已。

（7）閱讀時，應大膽猜字，推敲上下文的意思，以掌握文章要義。

（8）應考時，應「不求甚解」，以免因小失大。亦即不要非把所有單字片語弄懂不可，而應把焦點放在如何答對更多的題目上面。

（9）提升自己的閱讀速度，以便能有充裕時間思考及檢查。

（10）注意時間的掌握，切勿慌亂中作答。

(11) 多做模擬試題，以知己知彼，並對症下藥。

(12) 作答時，勿在某一題目上停留過久。一般思考兩次後仍不得其解時，即須斷然離開，往下作答，待最後再回頭與之對決。

(13) 以消去法作答。但如果選項只剩兩個而不知如何取決時，則隨便抓一個。

(14) 依直覺作答。依作者經驗，作答後仍猶豫其解，最後再更改答案者，常會後悔莫及，甚至痛不欲生。

(15) 預留一分鐘時間，把所有不會寫的題目猜完並記得塗黑答案卡。

(16) 寫閱讀測驗題組作答時，須先快速瀏覽題目，以便在文章中快速找到答案。一般初級英檢的答案會明顯出現在文章中。

(17) 加強字彙的記憶。至少要熟記教育部公布之「英語常用2000字」才能應付初級測驗。

(18) 熟記文法要點及句型：如五大基本句型、時態、假設語氣、連接詞、子句、被動語態、比較級、不定詞、動名詞等。

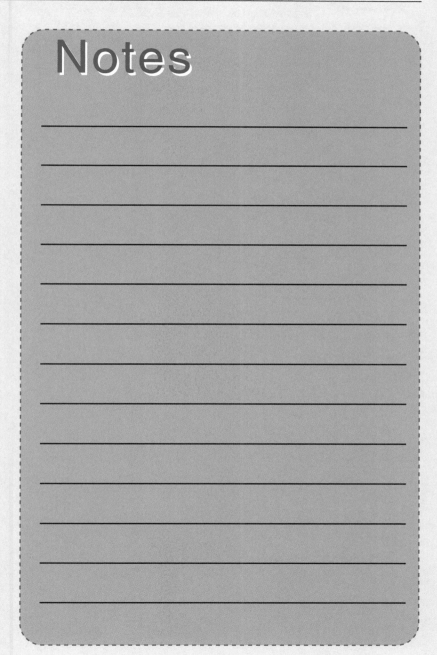

Notes

第二章 文法要點

1 一招半式闖江湖──五大基本句型

【第一式】**S + V**（主詞＋動詞）

① She smiled.
她微笑。

② He runs fast.
他跑得快。

③ It rained heavily last night.
昨晚雨下得很大。

【第二式】**S + V + C**（主詞＋動詞＋補語）

① The fruit tastes sweet.
這水果嚐起來很甜。

② She became a writer.
她成為作家。

③ He is crazy.
他瘋了。

【第三式】**S + V + O**（主詞＋動詞＋受詞）

① I hate you.
我恨你。

② He killed himself.
他自殺了。

③ They didn't answer my question.
他們沒有回答我的問題。

【第四式】**S + V + I.O. + D.O.**（主詞＋動詞＋間接受詞＋直接受詞）

① I gave Joe a comic book
   我給 Joe 一本漫畫書。

② Show me your ID.
   把證件拿出來。（省略主詞 You）

③ I'll give you a call tonight.
   晚上打電話給你。

【第五式】**S + V + O + O.C.**（主詞＋動詞＋受詞＋受詞補語）

① The music made me sleepy.
   這音樂讓我想睡覺。

② We elected him chairman.
   我們選他當主席。

③ Don't drive me crazy.
   別把我逼瘋。（省略主詞 you）

2 名詞與代名詞

壹、名詞

【說明】

> 名詞就是人、事、物,一般分為五類:普通名詞、集合名詞、專有名詞、物質名詞、抽象名詞。

（1）普通名詞:

可當單複數,如 apple, pen, bus, party 等。

① I like apples (the) most/best.

我最喜歡蘋果。

② There are two parties tonight.

今晚有兩個派對。

③ You need to change buses to get there.

你必須換車才能到那裡。

※ 單數變複數規則:

一般 → + s:apple → apples;pen → pens

字尾 s, ch, sh, x → + es:bus → buses;watch → watches;brush → brushes;box → boxes

字尾子音 + o → + es:hero → heroes;tomato → tomatoes;potato → potatoes

字尾子音 + y → 去 y 加 ies:party → parties;city → cities

字尾母音 + y → + s:day → days;boy → boys

（2）集合名詞:

表示一個單位的群體或被視為整體的人、事、物,如 people, class, family, team, police(警方)等。

① There are many people in the park.

公園裡有很多人。

② We are family.

　我們是一家人。

（3）專有名詞：

指特定的人、物、地方，如John, Brown, March, Taipei, Sunday, Mr.等。

① I went to Taipei to visit John in March.

　三月時我去台北找 John。

② Are you going shopping with the Browns?

　你要和 Brown 一家人去逛街嗎？

　※ the Browns ＝ the Brown family：指 Brown 一家人。

（4）物質名詞：

指沒有固定形狀的物質，包括氣體、液體、材料、食物、礦物、金屬等，一律採用單數，如 air（空氣）、sugar（糖）、butter（奶油）、meat（肉）、metal（金屬）、glass（玻璃）、flour（麵粉）、iron（鐵）、wood（木頭）、salt（鹽）等。

① Please give me some sugar.

　請給我一些糖。

② Glass breaks easily.

　玻璃易碎。

（5）抽象名詞：

表示觀念、性質、狀況等事物，一般用單數，如 love, honesty, happiness 等。

① You can't buy love with money.

　你無法用金錢買到愛情。

② Honesty is the best policy.

　誠實為上策。

貳、代名詞

【說明】

代名詞就是你、我、他，但細分則有五類：人稱代名詞、指示代名詞、不定代名詞、疑問代名詞、關係代名詞。

（1）人稱代名詞：

區別說話者、對話者及第三者之代名詞，共分為第一人稱（I, we）、第二人稱（you），及第三人稱（he, she, it, they），各有單複數，作主詞用。

	主格	受格	所有格	所有格代名詞
我	I	me	my	mine
你	you	you	your	yours
他	he	him	his	his
她	she	her	her	hers
它	it	it	its	its
我們	we	us	our	ours
你們	you	you	your	yours
他們	they	them	their	theirs

① **His** father is sick.
他父親生病了。

② **He** told **us** a joke.
他講了一個笑話給我們聽。

③ The two dogs are **theirs**.
這兩隻狗是他們的。

（2）指示代名詞：

指人、事、物之代名詞，如 this, that, these, those 等。

① That's my English teacher.
那是我的英文老師。

② These are mine.
這些東西是我的。

（3）不定代名詞：

指不特定的人、事、物，如 any, each, both, neither, something, nothing, somebody, nobody 等。

① Nobody is perfect.
沒有人是完美的。

② **Neither** of the sisters **is** married.
兩個**姊妹**都沒有**結婚**。

③ **Both** of them are **not** married.
他們兩個並非都結婚了。（即一個已婚，一個未婚）

④ Would you like something/anything to drink?
= Anything to drink?
你要喝點什麼嗎？

（4）疑問代名詞：

做為問句的代名詞，如 what, when, which, who, where 等。

① What do you want?
你要什麼？你要幹嘛？

② Which do you prefer, beef or pork?
你比較喜歡哪個，牛肉還是豬肉？

（5）關係代名詞：

具有名詞與連接詞功能的代名詞，如 who, which, where, that 等。

① The book **which** is on the desk is mine.
桌上那本書是我的。

② The man **who** lives next door is very friendly.
住在隔壁的那個男的很友善。

3 時態

不管是說是寫，只要英文一出，必含時態（tenses），這是中英文之間最大的不同，也是國人在使用英語時常會出錯的地方。例如：

（1）中文：他們昨天去博物館。

　　英文：They **went** to the museum yesterday.

（2）中文：他們常去博物館。

　　英文：They often **go** to the museum.

（3）中文：他們明天要去博物館。

　　英文：They **will go** to the museum tomorrow.

從以上的例子我們可以看出：中文不因時間改變而改變動詞的形式，亦即一個「去」字，便能跨越時空，行遍天下（不過，這得在華人地區喔！）。而英文則不然，若「去」博物館這個動作發生在過去，則動詞用「went」；若發生在現在，則用「go」（若主詞為第三人稱單數，即「他、她、它、牠」，則用 goes，其餘動詞大多加「s」）；若發生在未來，則用「will go」，不過這只是粗略的情況。若要細分，則英文時態共有十二種，即：

（1）現在簡單式　　（2）現在進行式

（3）現在完成式　　（4）現在完成進行式

（5）過去簡單式　　（6）過去進行式

（7）過去完成式　　（8）過去完成進行式

（9）未來簡單式　　（10）未來進行式

（11）未來完成式　　（12）未來完成進行式

壹、現在簡單式（**Simple Present Tense**）

【句型】S + V

使用時機

（1）表示目前的習慣：

① I usually get up at 6.

我通常六點起床。

② Nina often goes shopping with her sister.

Nina 常和她姊妹去逛街。

（2）表示不變的事實或真理：

① The sun rises in the east.

太陽從東邊升起。

② Experience is a good teacher.

經驗是良師。

（3）表示目前存在的事實：

① The book sells well.

這本書賣得好。

② She is a street vender.

她是個攤販。

（4）表示目前發生的頻率或次數：

① Judy goes to the movies once a week.

Judy 每週看一次電影。

② "How often do the buses run ?"

"Every 10 minutes."

「公車多久一班？」

「每十分鐘。」

（5）表示特性：

① She is very shy.

她很害羞。

② Glass bottles break easily.
玻璃瓶容易破。

（6）表示未來時間：

① The concert starts at 7:30 next Tuesday.
音樂會下週二七點半開始。

② You must go there before you leave tomorrow.
你明天離開之前，必須到那裡一趟。

貳、現在進行式（Present Continuous Tense）

【句型】 **S + be + V-ing**

| 使用時機

（1）表示在說話時，正在進行的事件、動作或行為：

① Andy is studying for the test now.
Andy 正在準備考試。

② They are surfing the net.
他們正在上網。

（2）表示暫時的情況：

① I'm living with my parents until I get married.
結婚前我都會住在家裡。

② The department store is having a sale this week.
這家百貨公司本週有特賣會。

（3）表示預定之計畫：

① They're getting married next week.
他們下個禮拜結婚。

② I'm spending my next vacation in Japan.
我下次要到日本渡假。

參、現在完成式（Present Perfect Tense）

【句型】S + have/has + p.p.（過去分詞）

使用時機

（1）表示過去動作所造成的現在結果：

① I have cleaned the table. (So it's clean now.)
我已經清好桌子。（所以它現在是乾淨的）

② They have widened the road. (So it's wide now.)
他們已拓寬馬路。（所以它現在是寬的）

（2）表示前不久才發生的事情，或剛完成的動作，常與 **just** 連用：

① I've just finished my homework.
我剛寫完功課。

② He has just arrived from Hong Kong.
他剛從香港抵達這裡。

（3）表示截至目前為止的經驗：

① They have visited Taiwan five times.
他們來台灣已有五次之多。

② This is the first time he has driven a car.
這是他第一次開車。

③ It's the most boring movie I've ever seen.
這是我看過最無聊的電影。

（4）表示一段尚在持續的時間（如 **today**）內所發生的事件、動作
或行為：

① Jessie has eaten nothing today.
Jessie 今天還沒有吃東西。

② I haven't seen your cat this week.
我這個星期還沒有看到你的貓。

（5）表示預期中的事件、動作或行為，常用於否定句及疑問句，並
　　　與 yet（尚，還）連用：

　　　① She hasn't finished her homework yet.
　　　　她還沒有寫完功課。

　　　② A: "Have you washed your hair yet?"
　　　　B: "Not yet."
　　　　A：你洗頭了沒？
　　　　B：還沒。

（6）表示從過去到現在一段時間內所發生的事件、動作或行為，常
　　　與 already（已經）、ever（曾經）、never（從未）、before（從
　　　前）、so far（至今）、up to now（至今）、(up) till now（至今）、
　　　up to the present（至今）、recently（最近）、lately（最近）、
　　　of late = lately, in the last few years（在最近幾年）、in the past
　　　three days（在過去三天）、since（自從）、for（長達）等連用：

　　　① I have never tasted kiwi fruit (before).
　　　　我從未吃過奇異果。

　　　② The boss has gone out (already).
　　　　= The boss has (already) gone out.
　　　　老闆已經出去了。

　　　③ Have you ever been to Korea (before)?
　　　　你曾去過韓國嗎？

　　　④ We haven't heard from Bill so far.
　　　　我們至今仍沒有 Bill 的消息。

　　　⑤ They have traveled around the island lately.
　　　　他們最近去環島旅行。

　　　⑥ Taiwan has made great progress in the last ten years.
　　　　台灣在最近十年有長足的進步。

（7）since 與 for 的用法：

【句型】
$$S + have/has + p.p. + since + \begin{cases} 過去定點時間 \\ S + V 過去式 \end{cases}$$

$$S + have/has + p.p. + for + 時間長度$$

① She hasn't written to me since March.

　她從三月以來就沒寫信給我。

② We've known each other since we were eight or nine.

　我們打從八、九歲就認識到現在。

③ My father has stopped drinking for three years.

　= My father has stopped drinking since three years ago.

　我父親戒酒已三年了。

（8）have been 與 have gone 的區別：

① I have been to Hong Kong.

　我曾去過香港。

② He has gone to Japan (already).

　他已經去日本了。

③ We've never been there (before).

　我們不曾到過那裡。

肆、現在完成進行式（Present Perfect Continuous Tense）

【句型】S + have/has + been + V-ing

■ 使用時機

（1）表示過去某動作持續到現在，並且仍繼續進行著：

① I have been studying English for a long time.

　我學英文已經很久了。

② She has been watching TV since 2 o'clock in the afternoon.

　她從下午兩點看電視一直看到現在。

③ A: "How long have you been working here?"

　B: "Since 1980."

　A：你在這裡工作多久了？

　B：從一九八〇年開始。

伍、過去簡單式（ **Simple Past Tense** ）

【句型】**S + p.t.** （動詞過去式）

▌ 使用時機

表示發生在過去的事件、動作或行為，**通常與過去時間**，如 **last night, yesterday, two years ago** 等連用。

① I went to a concert last night.
　昨晚我去聽音樂會。

② He killed himself yesterday.
　他昨天自殺了。

③ Tom died two years ago.
　Tom 兩年前去世。
　= Tom has been dead for two years.
　Tom 已經死了兩年。

④ She overslept this morning.
　她今天早上睡過頭。

⑤ They were hurt in a car accident the other day.
　他們前幾天車禍受傷。

陸、過去進行式（ **Past Continuous Tense** ）

【句型】**S + was/were + V-ing**

▌ 使用時機

（1）表示過去某特定時間內正在進行的事件、動作或行為：

　① This time last year she was selling pearl milk tea.
　　去年此時她在賣珍珠奶茶。

　② I was taking a shower at eleven o'clock last night.
　　昨晚十一點我正在洗澡。

（2）表示過去某動作發生時，另一個動作正在進行之中，亦即過去
　　的兩個動作，進行時間較長者用過去進行式，進行時間較短者
　　用過去簡單式。

　　① She was sleeping upstairs when the fire broke out.
　　　 = The fire broke out while she was sleeping upstairs.
　　　 火災發生時，她正在樓上睡覺。

　　② When John arrived, we were having dinner.
　　　 John 到的時候，我們正在吃晚飯。

柒、過去完成式（Past Perfect Tense）

【句型】S + had + p.p.

┃ 使用時機

（1）過去兩事件先發生者用過去完成式，後發生者用過去簡單式：

　　① When I got to the station, the train had already left.
　　　 當我到車站時，火車已經走了。

　　② I didn't go to the movie last night because I had seen it
　　　 before.
　　　 我昨晚沒去看電影，因為我已經看過了。

（2）在過去某定點時間之前所完成的事件、動作或行為：

　　① The rain had stopped by two yesterday afternoon.
　　　 雨下到昨天下午兩點就停了。

　　② They had stopped quarreling by six o'clock when dinner was
　　　 ready.
　　　 他們到了六點要吃晚飯時才停止爭吵。

捌、過去完成進行式（Past Perfect Continuous Tense）

【句型】**S + had + been + V-ing**

使用時機

表示一個持續到過去某個定點時間的事件、動作或行為：

① How long **had you been waiting** before the bus **came**?
  你等了多久公車才來？

② **I had been waiting** for two hours when the train **arrived**.
  火車到的時候，我已經等了兩個小時。

玖、未來簡單式（Future Tense）

【句型1】**S + will + V原形**

使用時機

（1）表示發生在未來的事件、動作或行為：

  ① I will stay with my uncle tonight.
    今晚我要住在叔叔家。

  ② She will arrive in Japan next Monday.
    她下星期一將抵達日本。

（2）表示對將來所作的預言：

  ① It will rain cats and dogs tomorrow.
    明天會下大雨。

    ※ rain cats and dogs = rain heavily

  ② There will be a typhoon next week.
    下週將會有颱風。

（3）表示允諾或意圖：
　　① I'll take it.
　　　 我要這個。我要買。我接受。
　　② I'll buy you dinner after work.
　　　 下班後我請你吃飯。

（4）表示要求或邀請：
　　① Will you hold the phone, please?
　　　 請稍後，好嗎？
　　② Will you be my guest tonight?
　　　 今天晚上當我的座上賓好嗎？

（5）表示正式宣布的事件：
　　① The wedding will take place at St. Patrick's on May 6.
　　　 婚禮將在五月六日於聖派屈克教堂舉行。
　　② The school sports will be held next Sunday.
　　　 學校運動會將於下週日舉行。

【句型2】S + be + going to + V原形
▌ 使用時機
表示意願或計劃好將來要做的事情：
① We're going to play three-on-three this afternoon.
　 今天下午我們要去玩三對三鬥牛賽。
② Are you going to have a party in your house?
　 你要在你們家辦派對嗎？

【句型3】S + be + V-ing

▌使用時機

（1）來去動詞，如 come, go, arrive, leave, fly 等，可用進行式代
替未來式：

① My uncle is coming tomorrow.
我叔叔明天要來。

② I'm flying to Bali this evening.
今天晚上我要搭機去峇里島。

（2）表示已經安排好要做的事：

① He is washing his car this afternoon.
他今天下午要洗車。

② We are getting married next Sunday.
我們下週日結婚。

【句型4】S + V

▌使用時機

（1）表示時間表或節目表：

① The train leaves Taipei at 9:30 and arrives in Taichung at
11:30.
火車九點半從台北發車，十一點半抵達台中。

② What time does the show begin ?
表演幾點開始？

（2）主要子句表未來時，副詞子句用現在式代替未來式：

① I'll wait here until he comes back.
我要在這裡等到他回來。

② Before you leave tomorrow, you must try the pearl milk tea.
你明天離開前，一定要去嚐一下珍珠奶茶。

③ I'll give you a call as soon as I **get** there.

我一到那裡就打電話給你。

④ When the rain **stops**, we will go roller-blading.

雨停的時候，我們就要去溜直排輪。

⑤ If she **does not** come soon, I will not wait any longer.

如果她不快來，我就不再等了。

拾、未來進行式（**Future Continuous Tense**）

【句型】**S + will + be + V-ing**

┃ 使用時機

（1）表示在未來某定點時間或一段時間內正在進行的事件、動作或

行為：

① We will probably be having dinner when you come tomorrow.

明天你來的時候，我們可能正在吃晚餐。

② I'll be watching news on TV between 7 and 8 tonight.

今晚七點到八點間，我會看電視新聞。

（2）表示已經安排好要去做的事情：

① I will be doing the laundry this afternoon.

= I am going to do the laundry this afternoon.

= I'm doing the laundry this afternoon.

今天下午我要洗衣服。

② Don't call me this evening. I'll be watching the ball game.

今天晚上別打電話給我，我要看球賽。

拾壹、未來完成式（Future Perfect Tense）

【句型】S + will + have + p.p.

使用時機

表示在未來某定點時間之前所完成的動作、行為或事件：

① He will have finished his work by six.
　　六點前他會完成工作。

② I won't have read all of it until the weekend.
　　我要到週末才有辦法全部唸完。

拾貳、未來完成進行式（Future Perfect Continuous Tense）

【句型】S + will + have + been + V-ing

使用時機

表示到未來某定點時間仍持續進行的事件、動作或行為，其動詞常用 work, wait, live, study 等：

① I'll have been studying English for ten years by September.
　　到九月的時候，我英文就已經唸了十年了。

② They will have been arguing for three hours if they don't stop by now.
　　如果到現在還沒有停止的話，那他們就已經吵了三個小時了。

【句型】 S + used to + V原形　表示過去的習慣或事實

　　　　 S + be used to + V-ing/N　表示現在已習以為常

① I used to play basketball a lot, but now I'm too busy.

我以前常打籃球，但現在太忙了。

② He is not what he used to be.

= He is not what he was.

他已經不是以前的他了。（今非昔比）

③ My mom is used to getting up early.

我媽習慣早起。

④ Don't worry. You'll get/be used to it in no time.

別擔心，你很快就會習慣了。

⑤ Did you use to go hiking when you were little?

你小時候常去健行嗎？

⑥ Tourists didn't use to come here.

觀光客以前不常來這裡。

4 疑問句及附加問句

壹、疑問句

【說明】

疑問句通常用來詢問一個敘述是否屬實，或對敘述表示質疑。

【句型1】 **Be + S + C（補語）?**
　　　　 Be + S + V-ing (now)?

① Is she a musician?
　她是音樂家嗎？

② Am I pretty?
　我好看嗎？

③ Are you American?（勿用 an American）
　你是美國人嗎？

④ Is it an apple tree?
　那是蘋果樹嗎？

⑤ Are they chicken?
　他們是不是很膽小？
　※ **chicken**：膽小的，膽小鬼。

⑥ Were you at the movies last night?
　你昨晚去看電影嗎？
　※ **movies = movie theater**：戲院。

⑦ Are you watching TV (now)?
　你在看電視嗎？

⑧ Were you sleeping when I called you last night?
　昨晚我打電話給你時，你正在睡覺嗎？
　※ **Be** 動詞適用對象：
　　am → I

is → he, she, it, 單數名詞

are → we, you, they, 複數名詞

was（過去式）→ I, he, she, it, 單數名詞

were（過去式）→ we, you, they, 複數名詞

【句型2】 Be + there + N（名詞）?

① Is there a laundromat near here?
這裡附近有洗衣店嗎？

② Are there any mistakes in this report?
這份報告有任何錯誤嗎？

③ Was there any money in the wallet?
那皮夾裡有錢嗎？

④ Were there any mistakes in his paper?
他的試卷／報告有任何錯誤嗎？

【句型3】 Do/Does + S + V原形?

| 說　明

主詞為第三人稱單數（如 he, she, it）或單數名詞（如 the boy），則以
Does 開頭，其餘以 Do 開頭。

① Do you have a credit card?
你有信用卡嗎？

② Do I have any choice?
我有選擇的權利嗎？

③ Do we have to do this?
我們非做不可嗎？

④ Do they know how to drive?
他們會開車嗎？

⑤ Do the buses run very often?

= Does the bus run very often?

車班多嗎？

⑥ Does she speak Taiwanese?

她會講台語嗎？

⑦ Does he have a brother?

他有兄弟嗎？

⑧ Does your dog bite?

你的狗會咬人嗎？

【句型4】 **Did + S + V**原形**?** （用於過去式）

｜ 說　明

過去事件不管主詞為第幾人稱或單複數，皆以 Did 開頭。

① Did you sleep well last night?

你昨晚睡得好嗎？

② Did they win the game?

他們比賽贏了嗎？

③ Did I tell you about it?

我有告訴你這件事嗎？

【句型5】

Can/May/Shall/Will/Must/Need/Dare + S + V原形**?**

① Can I help you?

有什麼事嗎？需要服務嗎？

② May I speak to Derek, please?

請問 Derek 在嗎？（用於通話）

③ Shall we eat out tonight?

今天晚上要上館子嗎?

④ Will you (please) be quiet?

= Will you be quiet, please?

= Be quiet, will you?

請安靜好嗎?

⑤ Must I fill out the form?

= Do I have to fill out the form?

我必須填這份表格嗎?

⑥ Need he come?

= Does he need to come?

他需要過來嗎?

⑦ Dare you talk back to your father?

= Do you dare to talk back to your father?

你敢向你父親回嘴嗎?

【句型6】 Could/Might/Should/Would + S + V?

① Could I possibly use your car?

能否借用你的車?

※ 加 possibly 比較委婉。

② Might I sit here?(較正式)

我可以坐這裡嗎?

③ Should we invite Susan to our wedding?

我們該邀請Susan來參加婚禮嗎?

④ Would you show me the way to the station (, please)?

請問車站怎麼走?

【句型7】 Have/Has/Had + S + p.p. (yet)?

┃ 說　明

此為完成式句型（詳見「時態」），第三人稱單數助動詞用 **has**，其餘用 **have**，而若事件發生在過去，則一律用 **had**。

① Have you washed your hair yet?
　你洗過頭了沒？

② Have you ever been here (before)?
　你曾來過這裡嗎？

③ Has John finished his project?
　John 已經完成他的計畫了嗎？

④ Has she been sick lately?
　她最近生病了嗎？

⑤ Had he gone when you came?
　你來的時候他是不是已經走了？

【句型8】 Wh-word + be + C?
　　　　 Wh-word + be + V-ing?

┃ 說　明

Wh-word 在此當主詞，Wh-word 包括 What, Who, Which, When, Where。

① What's wrong?
　= What's the matter?
　= What's going on (here)?
　怎麼了？發生什麼事？

② Who is better?
　誰比較好？

③ Which is worse, John or Tom?
　哪一個比較差，是 John 還是 Tom？

④ What's so funny?
= What are you laughing for?
= Why are you laughing?
有什麼好笑的？你笑什麼？
⑤ Who is in charge (here)?
這裡是誰負責的？
⑥ Who is singing?
誰在唱歌？
⑦ What's happening?
= What's up?
近來如何？怎麼了？發生什麼事？

【句型9】 Wh-word + V?
　　　　 Wh-word + V + O (+ C)?
① What happened?
發生什麼事？
② Who died?
誰死了？
③ Who did it?
誰幹的？
④ What brings you here?
是什麼風把你吹來的？
⑤ What makes you think so?
你為何如此認為？

【句型10】 Wh-word + have/has/had + S + p.p.?
① What have I done?
我做（錯）了什麼？

② What has she said?
　她說了什麼？
③ When had he gone?
　他什麼時候離開的？

【句型11】　Wh-word + be + S...?
　　　　　　Wh-word + be + S + V-ing...?

① Who is that big guy?
　那個大塊頭是誰？
　※ guy = man
② What is he?
　= What does he do?
　= What's his occupation/job?
　他是做什麼的？
③ What's the rush?
　急什麼？（幹嘛那麼急？）
④ Where are you from?
　= Where do you come from?
　你是哪裡人？
⑤ What are you here for?
　你來這裡做什麼？
⑥ Where are you going?
　你要去哪裡？
⑦ What are you talking about?
　你在說什麼？（你在胡說些什麼？）
⑧ When are you leaving?
　= When do you leave?
　你什麼時候走？
⑨ How are you doing?（較口語）
　= How are you?
　= How's it going?
　你好嗎？

【句型12】 **Wh-word + Aux**（助動詞）**+ S + V**（**+ O + C**）**?**

① What do you want?

你要什麼東西？你要做什麼？

② What did you say?

= Pardon (me)?

= I'm sorry?

= Excuse me?

= I beg your pardon?

你說什麼？

※ 以上句子語調要上揚。

③ What do you mean (by that)?

你說這話什麼意思？

④ When can I see you again?

何時能再見到你？

⑤ How do I get to the station?

火車站怎麼走？

※ **get to**：到達。

⑥ How would you like your steak (cooked)?

牛排要幾分熟？

⑦ Why did he do that?

他為什麼那麼做呢？

⑧ Who do you want to speak to?

你要找哪位？（電話中）

【句型13】 **Wh-word**（**+ N**）**+ have/has/had + p.p.?**

　　　　　 Wh-word（**+ N**）**+ have/has/had + p.p. + O?**

① What's happened?

發生了什麼事？

※ **What's = What has**

② Who has done this?

= Who's done it?

是誰幹的？

※ Who's = Who has

③ Who had (already) run away before the police came?
警方來之前，誰已先開溜？

④ Which story has interested you (the) most?
哪一個故事最令你感到興趣？

【句型14】 **Wh-word + N + be + C?**
Wh-word + N + be + V-ing（+ O）?

① Which car is better?
哪一部車比較好？

② Whose English is worse?
誰的英文比較差？

③ Which one is running faster?
哪一部跑得比較快？

※ ①～③ 句為比較級，用法詳見文法比較級。

④ Which doctor is helping your father?
哪一位醫生在幫你爸爸的忙？

【句型15】 **Wh-word + N + V?**
Wh-word + N + V + O（+ C）?

① Which team won?
哪一隊贏了？

② Whose grandfather died?
誰的祖父死了？

③ What disease killed him?
他死於何種疾病？

④ What news makes you so excited?
什麼消息讓你如此興奮？

【句型16】 **Wh-word + N + be + S?**
　　　　　　 Wh-word + N + be + S + V-ing?

① What size are you?
你的尺寸為何？（用於購物時）

② What date is today?
= What's the date today?
今天幾號？

③ What day is (it) today?
今天星期幾？

④ Whose bike is this?
這輛腳踏車是誰的？

⑤ What program are you watching (now)?
你現在在看什麼節目？

⑥ Which horse are you studying?
你在研究哪一匹馬？

【句型17】 **Wh-word + N + Aux**（助動詞）**+ S + V（+ O）？**
　　　　　 介系詞 + Wh-word + N + Aux + S + V（+ O）？

① What time does the next train leave?
下班火車幾點開？

② What brand do you want?
你要什麼牌子的？

③ Which restaurant do you recommend?
你推薦哪家餐廳？

④ Which way should we go?
我們該走哪一條路？

⑤ On which floor do you live?
你住幾樓？

⑥ In which restaurant did you have your Christmas dinner?
= Where did you have your Christmas dinner?
你的耶誕大餐是在哪家餐廳吃的？

▌補　充

疑問詞 **how** 的其他用法：

① "How often do you play basketball?"
　　"Once a week."
　　「你多久打一次籃球？」
　　「一星期一次。」

② "How many times have you visited Hong Kong?"
　　"About four or five times."
　　「你去過香港幾次？」
　　「大概四、五次。」

③ "How much do you weigh?"
　　"About 150 pounds."
　　「你多重？」
　　「大約一百五十磅。」

④ "How much sugar do you need?"
　　"About two pounds."
　　「你需要多少糖？」
　　「大概兩磅。」

⑤ "How long will the meeting last?"
　　"About three hours."
　　「會議要開多久？」
　　「大概三小時。」

⑥ "How tall are you?"
　　"I'm six feet tall."
　　「你多高？」
　　「我身高六呎。」

⑦ "How long is the ride?"
　　"About 40 minutes."
　　「車程多遠？」
　　「大概四十分鐘。」

⑧ "How far is the nearest gas station?"
"It's about two miles away."
「最近的加油站離這裡多遠？」
「大約兩英哩。」

※　其他相關用法可參考<u>副詞子句</u>和<u>形容詞子句</u>。

貳、附加問句

【說明】

在一個敘述句之後，附加一個簡略問句，此簡略問句稱為附加問句（亦即在口語英文中，放在句尾的短問句），其功能在詢問對方是否贊同這個敘述。

《用法》

（1）在肯定敘述句之後，我們用否定形式的附加問句，來詢問對方是否贊同這個敘述。

（2）在否定敘述句之後，我們用肯定形式的附加問句，來詢問對方是否贊同這個敘述，而這往往也傳達一種驚訝的情緒。

（3）在肯定敘述之後，我們有時也可用肯定形式的附加問句來查詢某個訊息是否正確，而這也往往表現出一種興趣、關心、憤怒或好奇心。

（4）敘述句和附加問句的主詞相同，只是後者主詞須用代名詞。

（5）在含 let's 的句型中，我們用含 shall 之附加問句。

（6）在命令句之後，我們用含 will, would, can 或 could 之附加問句。

《唸法》

（1）當我們很不確定自己的敘述是否正確時，附加問句用上升語調。

（2）當我們確定自己的敘述是正確的，且欲詢問對方是否贊同時，附加問句用下降語調。

【句型1】 S + be..., be-n't + S?
　　　　　（但 I am..., am I not/aren't I?）

> ※ be = am, is, are, was, were
>
> be-n't = isn't, aren't, wasn't, weren't

① It's a beautiful day, **isn't it?**
天氣很好，不是嗎？

> ※ 口語常省略 **It's a**，亦即改為 **Beautiful day, isn't it?**

② You're American, **aren't you?**
你是美國人，不是嗎？

③ I'm on the list, **am I not?**
= I'm on the list, aren't I?
我在名單上，不是嗎？

④ She's very proud, **isn't she?**
她很驕傲，不是嗎？

⑤ John is a lawyer, **isn't he?**
John 是個律師，不是嗎？

⑥ We **are** in the same class, **aren't we?**
我們在同一個班級，不是嗎？

⑦ You guys **are** from Taiwan, **aren't you?**
你們是台灣來的，不是嗎？

> ※ **you guys**：你們。屬流行口語，**guy(s)** 可指男或男女一群人，女的
> 則用 **gal(s)**。

⑧ They're in the gym, **aren't they?**
他們在體育館，不是嗎？

⑨ You **were** at Jim's party last night, **weren't you?**
你昨天去參加 Jim 的派對，不是嗎？

⑩ She **was** hurt in the car accident, **wasn't she?**
她車禍受傷，不是嗎？

⑪ They **were** fighting, **weren't they?**
他們那時在打架，不是嗎？

⑫ I was cheated, wasn't I?
我被騙了，不是嗎？

⑬ They are working at a bank, aren't they?
他們現在在銀行上班，不是嗎？

⑭ You're fixing the car, aren't you?
你在修車，不是嗎？

⑮ The food is delicious, isn't it?
這食物很好吃，不是嗎？

⑯ It was a great movie, wasn't it?
它是一部很棒的電影，不是嗎？

【句型2】 S + V, don't/doesn't + S?
　　　　 S + V過去式, didn't + S?

　　　　　　※ 第三人稱單數用 doesn't，其餘用 don't。

① You like this weather, don't you?
你喜歡這樣的天氣，不是嗎？

② James works hard, doesn't he?
James 工作認真，不是嗎？

③ You enjoyed the movie, didn't you?
你很喜歡這部電影，不是嗎？

④ He went to Hong Kong last Sunday, didn't he?
他上個星期天去香港，不是嗎？

【句型3】 **There + is/are + N, isn't/aren't there?**（表現在式）
　　　　　 There was/were + N, wasn't/weren't there?（表過去式）

　　　　※ **there** 可當主詞。

① There is a movie theater around here, **isn't there**?
　 這附近有家戲院，不是嗎？

② There are two supermarkets in the neighborhood, **aren't there**?
　 這附近有兩家超市，不是嗎？

③ There was a lot of traffic, **wasn't there**?
　 車輛很多，不是嗎？

④ There were lots of people at the party, **weren't there**?
　 派對很熱鬧（人很多），不是嗎？

【句型4】 **S + will/can/must + V原形, won't/can't/mustn't + S?**

① You'll be there, **won't you**?
　 你會去的，不是嗎？

② We'll go on a picnic next week, **won't we**?
　 我們下週要去野餐，不是嗎？

③ Johnny will be here soon, **won't he**?
　 Johnny 很快就會到，不是嗎？

④ There will be a thunderstorm tomorrow, **won't there**?
　 明天會有暴風雨，不是嗎？

⑤ You can speak Japanese, **can't you**?
　 你會說日語，不是嗎？

⑥ You must go to class tomorrow, **mustn't you**?
　 你明天必須去上課，不是嗎？

　　※ mustn't〔`mʌsn̩t〕

【句型5】S + would/could/should + V原形, wouldn't/couldn't/
　　　　 shouldn't + S?
　　　　 S + had better + V原形, hadn't + S?

① You **would** like to work for him, **wouldn't you**?
　 你想要替他工作,不是嗎?
　 ※ **You would = You'd**

② You **would** hit the robber if you saw him, **wouldn't you**?
　 如果你看到搶匪,你會揍他,不是嗎?

③ Your mom **could** go to the hospital by herself, **couldn't she**?
　 你媽可以一個人去醫院,不是嗎?

④ You **should** help your mother in the house, **shouldn't you**?
　 你應該幫你媽做家事,不是嗎?

⑤ You'd rather stay here, **wouldn't you**?
　 你寧願待在這裡,不是嗎?
　 ※ **You'd = You would**

⑥ You'd **better** do it now, **hadn't you**?
　 你最好現在就去做,不是嗎?
　 ※ **You'd = You had**

【句型6】S + have/has + p.p., haven't/hasn't + S?
　　　　 S + had + p.p., hadn't + S?

① You **have been** to Japan, **haven't you**?
　 你去過日本,不是嗎?

② Judy **has passed** her driving test, **hasn't she**?
　 Judy 已經通過駕駛考試,不是嗎?

③ We **have seen** that movie already, **haven't we**?
　 我們已經看過那部電影,不是嗎?

④ The train **had already left** when you got there, **hadn't it**?
　 你到的時候,火車已經開了,不是嗎?

【句型7】 **Let's + V原形, shall we?**

Let us + V原形, will you?

Let's not + V原形, OK/all right?

① Let's go shopping, shall we?

= Shall we go shopping?

我們去逛街，好嗎？

② Let us go bowling, will you?

我們去打保齡球，好嗎？

③ Let's not argue any more, OK?

我們不要再爭辯了，好嗎？

【句型8】 **V, will/would you?** 表示請求之祈使句

V, won't/can't you? 表示客氣或不悅之祈使句

Don't + V, will you? 此為否定祈使句

① Give me a hand, will you?

= Would/Could/Will/Can you give me a hand?

幫個忙好嗎？

② Do me a favor, would you?

= Would/Could/Will/Can you do me a favor?

幫個忙好嗎？

③ Have a cookie, won't you?

= Won't you have a cookie?

= How about a cookie?

來塊餅乾，怎麼樣？

④ Don't treat me as a child, will you?

不要把我當小孩子對待，好嗎？

【句型9】 S + be + not..., be + S?

※ be = are, is, am, was, were

① You're not hungry, are you?

你不餓，是不是？

② They're not going out today, are they?

他們今天不出去，是不是？

③ Jack isn't on vacation now, is he?

Jack 現在沒有在渡假，是不是？

④ This isn't very funny, is it?

這不是很好笑，是不是？

⑤ There isn't much pollution around here, is there?

這附近沒有很多污染，是不是？

⑥ I wasn't wrong about you, was I?

我沒有誤會你，是不是？

⑦ You weren't listening, were you?

你剛剛沒有在聽，是不是？

⑧ There wasn't a lot of traffic this morning, was there?

今天早上交通不是很擁擠，是不是？

【句型10】 S + don't/doesn't + V, do/does + S?
　　　　　 S + didn't + V, did + S?

① You don't drink, do you?

你不喝酒，是不是？

② She doesn't know you, does she?

她不認識你，是不是？

③ I don't look well today, do I?

我今天氣色不好，是不是？

④ You don't think I'm innocent, do you?

你不認為我是無辜的，對不對？

⑤ You **didn't** go bowling yesterday, **did you**?
　你昨天沒有去打保齡球，是不是？
⑥ Ann **didn't** go to your wedding, **did she**?
　Ann 沒有去參加你的婚禮，是不是？

【句型11】 S + won't/can't/wouldn't/couldn't + V,
will/can/would/could + S?

① Kevin **won't** be late, **will he**?
　Kevin 不會遲到，是不是？
② You **couldn't** do me a favor, **could you**?
　你無法幫我的忙，是不是？
③ You **can't** cook, **can you**?
　你不會做飯，是不是？
④ You **wouldn't** give him a hand, **would you**?
　你不願意幫他，是不是？

【句型12】 S + have/has/had + not + p.p., have/has/had + S?

① You **haven't got** a pen, **have you**?
　你沒有筆，是嗎？
② She **hasn't gotten** up yet, **has she**?
　她還沒起床，是嗎？
③ He **hadn't prepared** for the test before he took it, **had he**?
　他考前沒有準備，是嗎？

5 助動詞

助動詞的範圍很廣，包括一般助動詞（be, have, do）及狀態助動詞（will, shall, can, may, must, need, dare, ought to）等等，當然這些助動詞的過去式，如 did, was, were, had, would, could, should, might 等等亦在此列。助動詞可幫助動詞，賦予句子不同的色彩，而形成不同的時態、語態、語法和語義。

《特色》

（１）助動詞後面的動詞要保持原形，亦即不加s或ed。

（２）兩個助動詞不可擺在一起，而須做些調整。例如：「一定能夠」不可寫成 must can，而須改成 must be able to。

（３）助動詞有多重意義，而有些助動詞其部分意義可相通。例如：can = may（可以），may = might = could（可能）。

（４）助動詞加not則成否定句，例如：

① I do not like ice cream.
我不喜歡冰淇淋。

② He could not come to the meeting.
他不能來參加會議。

（５）助動詞和主詞調換位置，亦即助動詞調至句首則成疑問句，例如：

① Do you live here ? ⟷ Don't you live here ?
你住在這裡嗎？⟷你不住在這裡嗎？

② Can you speak English ? ⟷ Can't you speak English ?
你會說英語嗎？⟷你不會說英語嗎？

（６）助動詞可放在句後而形成附加問句，例如：

① You like playing tennis, don't you ?

你喜歡打網球，不是嗎？

② You don't like cooking, do you ?

你不喜歡作菜，對不對？

（7）助動詞可形成簡答句，例如：

① A: Do you have a pen ?

B: Yes, I do. / No, I don't.

② A: I like swimming.

B: So do I.（我也是）

③ A: I don't know about that.

B: Neither/Nor do I.（我也不知道）

④ A: John speaks English very well.

B: So he does.（= Yes, he does. 沒錯。）

（8）避免重複而形成之省略句，例如：

① Judy doesn't often come to class, and when she **does**, she is usually late.

Judy 很少來上課，如果有來的話，通常也都會遲到。

② The rain might stop soon. On the other hand, it **might** not.

這雨可能不久就會停了，但也可能不會。

③ He likes ice cream, and I **do**, too.

他喜歡冰淇淋，而我也一樣。

（9）加強語氣，意為「真的，的確」，例如：

① I **do** like the puppy very much.

我真的很喜歡這隻小狗。

② She **did** break the window.

她的確有打破窗戶。

（10）否定副詞，如 hardly（幾乎不），scarcely（幾乎不）等須放在助動詞之後，例如：

① I can hardly wait to see you.

我迫不及待要見到你。

② The light is so dim that we can hardly see.

光線很暗，我們幾乎看不見。

壹、CAN

（1）表示能力：（= **be able to**）

① He can do the job very well.
他有能力把工作做好。

② We can beat them in the game.
我們可以在比賽中打敗他們。

③ I can't come to Tim's party tonight.
我無法參加今晚Tim辦的派對。

④ Judy is able to cook.
Judy 會做菜。

⑤ I'm able to do the job.
我會做那件工作。

（2）表示允許：（**can = may ; can't = mustn't**）

① You can come to my office tomorrow.
你明天可以來我辦公室。

② She can take a shower if she wants to.
她如果想洗澡，就去洗吧！

③ They can't smoke in the room.
他們不可以在房間內抽煙。

④ You can't drive in Taiwan if you're under 18.
在台灣未滿十八歲不准開車。

（3）表示徵求對方的同意：（**can = may ; can't = mustn't**）

① Can I speak to Allen, please?
= May I speak to Allen, please?
請 Allen 聽電話。（請問Allen在嗎？）

② Can you do me a favor?
能否幫個忙？

③ Can you please turn down the radio?

    = Will you please turn down the radio?

    = Could you please turn down the radio?（較客氣）

    = Would you please turn down the radio?（最客氣）

    請把收音機音量關小好嗎？

    ※ **please** 可以省略，不過加上去表示更客氣。

（4）表示主動提供協助：（ **can = may** ）

    ① Can I get you a cup of coffee？

      要不要來杯咖啡？

    ② Can I help you？

      = What can I do for you？

      需要幫忙嗎？請問有什麼事？

（5）表示對現在或未來所作的推論，或可能發生的事情：

    ① Can it be true？

      這會是真的嗎？

    ② Johnny can't be a playboy.

      Johnny 不可能是個花花公子。

    ③ You can see the lake from the bedroom window.

      從房間窗戶可以看到湖。

貳、COULD

（1）表示過去的能力，亦即 **can** 的過去式：（**= was/were able to**）

① My son could speak Taiwanese when he was two years old.
= My son was able to speak Taiwanese when he was two.
我兒子兩歲的時候就會講台語。

② They could play the piano when they were very young.
= They were able to play the piano when they were very young.
他們很小的時候就會彈鋼琴了。

③ I looked all over for the book, but I couldn't find it.
= I looked all over for the book, but I wasn't able to find it.
我到處找書，可是卻找不到。

┃ 注　意

如果要表示過去成功地完成某一具體動作，或在某特殊狀況下所展現出來的特殊能力，則須用 was/were able to，而不可用 could，如下例：

① The fire spread quickly, but everyone was able to escape.
火勢蔓延很快，不過每個人都逃了出來。

② I fell into the water, yet I was able to swim back at last.
我落水了，不過最後還是游了回來。

（2）表示提議：

① "What shall we do this evening?"
"We **could** go to the movies."
「晚上要做什麼？」
「我們可以去看電影。」

② When you go to L.A., you could stay with my uncle.
你去洛杉磯的時候，可以住我叔叔家。

（3）表示請求或同意：（**could = may = can = might**）

① Could I have the pepper, please?（比 can 客氣）

= May I have the pepper, please?（較尊重對方）

= Can I have the pepper, please?（最常用也最不正式）

= Might I have the pepper, please?（最客氣但最不常用）

能否給我胡椒粉呢？

② Excuse me. Could you tell me how to get to Taipei City Zoo?

對不起！請問台北市立動物園怎麼走？

※ **Could = Would**（最客氣）**= Will = Can**

③ Do you think you could (possibly) lend me some money?

= Do you think I could (possibly) borrow some money from you?

你可以借我錢嗎？

④ I wonder if you could help me.

不曉得你能不能幫個忙？

※ **if you could help me** 為名詞子句，用法詳見<u>子句</u>篇。

⑤ Could I possibly borrow your bike?

能否借用一下腳踏車？

※ 例句③④⑤語氣更加委婉。

（4）表示對目前及未來所作的推測，意為「可能」：（**could = might = may**）

① He could be right.

= He might be right.（較不肯定）

= He may be right.（較肯定）

他可能是對的。

② There could be another thunderstorm this evening.

今天晚上可能還有一場暴風雨。

（5）想像中的能力或能力的委婉表達：（**= would be able to**）

① I don't know how he works 16 hours a day. I couldn't do it.

我不曉得他怎麼能一天工作十六個小時，換作我可沒辦法喔！

② Why don't you apply for the job? You could get it.

你為什麼不去申請那份工作？你是有能力獲得的。

參、MAY

（**1**）表示許可：（**may = can**）
　① You may sit here.
　　你可以坐在這裡。
　② She may use this phone.
　　她可以用這支電話。
　③ You may not play badminton here.
　　你們不可以在這裡打羽毛球。

（**2**）表示請求：（**may = can = could = might**）
　① May I speak to Derek Chu, please?
　　可否請 Derek Chu 聽電話？
　② May/Can I help you?
　　= What can I do for you?
　　= How may/can I help you?
　　需要幫忙嗎？

（**3**）表示推測，意為「可能」：（可能性比 **might** 要高）
　① She may be in her office.
　　她可能在她辦公室。
　② I may go to the movies tonight.
　　我晚上可能會去看電影。
　③ Judy may not come to the wedding tonight. She isn't feeling very well.
　　Judy 晚上可能不會去參加婚禮，因為她身體不太舒服。
　④ Jack may be washing his car right now. He's going downtown tonight.
　　Jack 現在可能（正）在洗車，因為他晚上要去市區。
　⑤ Don't phone me at seven. I may be watching the news on TV.
　　七點不要打電話給我，因為我可能（正）在看電視新聞。

⑥ He may be going to Rome in November.

= He may go to Rome in November.

他十一月可能會去羅馬。

（4）表示願望、祝福：（may 可以省略）

【句型】**May + 對象 + V原形**

= (S) + wish + 對象 + N

① May you be happy forever.

願你永遠幸福快樂。

② May you be successful.

= May you succeed.

= Wish you success.

= I/We wish you success.

祝你成功。

③ May you have a good trip.

= Wish you a good trip.

= I/We wish you a good trip.

= Have a good trip.

祝你旅途愉快。

④ May God bless you.

= God bless you.

= Bless you.

願上帝保祐你。

※ 打噴嚏時，若有人對你說 **Bless you**，則應回答 **Thank you**，
反之亦然。

⑤ Long live the ROC.（倒裝句）

= (May) the ROC live long.

中華民國萬歲！

肆、MIGHT

（1）表示對現在或未來所作的推測，其可能性較 **may** 略低：

① It might rain this afternoon.
今天下午可能會下雨。

② He might be in the library.
他可能在圖書館。

③ They might be at the meeting.
他們可能在開會。

④ I might go to Japan in December.
我十二月可能會去日本。

（2）**might not**　可能不

① I might not go to the game tonight.
我今天晚上可能不去看球賽。

② Jean might not be in her office.
Jean可能不在她辦公室。

（3）**might + be + V-ing**　可能正在…（此為 **might** 與進行式之結合）

① Helen might be watching TV (right now).
Helen現在可能在看電視。

② They might be having a good time.
他們現在可能正玩得開心。

伍、MUST

（**1**）表示命令，意為「必須」，等於 **have/has to**，或 **have/has got to**
（語氣較強，老美較常用）：

① You must hurry (up).

= You have to hurry (up).

= You've got to hurry (up).

你必須快一點。

② He must study hard.

= He has to study hard.

= He's got to study hard.

他必須用功。

（**2**）**must not = mustn't**：表示強烈的禁止，意為「不准」，等於
may not, can not（語氣較弱）**, be not (going) to, shall not**
（語氣較強）：

① You mustn't smoke here.

你不准在此抽煙。

② Boys mustn't enter girls' dorms.

男生不准進入女生宿舍。

（**3**）表示對現在所作的肯定推斷，意為「一定，鐵定，必定」：

① He goes to the KTV every night. He must be an excellent
singer.

他每天晚上去 KTV，他一定是歌唱高手。

② Johnny knows a lot about movies. He must go to the movies
very often.

Johnny 很懂電影，他鐵定常去看電影。

陸、NEED

（1）**need to + V**原形　必須（**need** 在此作普通動詞用）

    ① She needs to see a doctor.

       = She has to see a doctor.

       她必須去看醫生。

    ② I need to take a break now.

       = I have to take a break now.

       = I need a break now.

       我現在需要休息一下。

    ③ Does she need to see a doctor?

       = Need she see a doctor?（need 在此為助動詞）

       她需要看醫生嗎？

    ④ I don't need to take a break.

       我不需要休息。

（2）**needn't + V**原形（**= don't/doesn't need to**）　不必，不須要
（針對現在或未來的事件或行為）

    ① You needn't hurry. You have plenty of time.

       = You don't need/have to hurry. You have plenty of time.

       = It's not necessary for you to hurry. You have plenty of time.

       你不必趕，你時間多得很。

    ② She needn't cry. Nobody will hurt her.

       = She doesn't need/have to cry. Nobody will hurt her.

       她不必要哭嘛！又沒有人會傷害她。

（3）**didn't need to + V**原形　無須、不必（針對過去的事件或行為）

    ① I didn't need to work yesterday.

       昨天我不必上班。

    ② She didn't need to go to the meeting, but she decided to go anyway.

       她不必去開會，但她還是決定去了。

柒、SHOULD

（**1**）表示義務或責任，意為「應該」（ **= ought to**）：

① You should help your mom in the house.

= You ought to help your mom in the house.

你應該幫媽媽做家事。

② The father should take care of the kid when the mother is gone.

媽媽走了以後，爸爸應該照顧小孩。

③ The government should do something about the pollution.

政府應該想辦法來解決污染問題。

④ One should love his country.

每個人都應該愛他的國家。

（**2**）表示提議、建議或勸誡，意為「應該」：

① Where should we go tonight?

= Where shall we go tonight?

今天晚上要去哪裡？

② You shouldn't drive so fast. You may get a ticket.

你不應該開這麼快，你會被開罰單的。

③ I think Tom should stop drinking.

我覺得 Tom 應該戒酒。

④ Should we invite Susie to the party?

= Shall we invite Susie to the party?

我們要不要邀 Susie 來參加派對呢？

⑤ Do you think I should apply for the job?

你認為我應該去應徵這份工作嗎？

（**3**）表示對現在或未來所作的預測：

① I should be home by nine.

我九點應該會到家。

② Jenny should pass her exam. She has been studying very hard.

Jenny 應該會通過考試的，因為她一直都很用功。

捌、WOULD

（**1**）表示客氣、委婉的陳述，或是想像的情況：

① Wednesday wouldn't be convenient for me.
  我禮拜三恐怕不太方便。

② That would seem (to be) a good idea.
  那個主意似乎還不錯。

③ I would guess the supermarkets are closed by now.
  我想超市現在應該關門了。

④ A holiday in Hawaii would be nice.
  到夏威夷渡假應該是很棒的。

（**2**）表示要求或邀請，語氣比**Could, Will, Can**要客氣：

① Would you wait a moment, please?
  = Could you wait a moment, please?
  = Will you wait a moment, please?
  = Can you wait a moment, please?
  能否請你等一下呢？

② Would you (please) leave me alone?
  能不能讓我靜一靜呢？

③ Would you be kind enough to open the door for me?
  = Would you be so kind as to open the door for me?
  = Would you please open the door for me?
  可以請你幫我把門打開嗎？

④ A: "Would you mind **turning** down the radio?"
  B: "No, I wouldn't." or "Not at all." or "Certainly not."
    or "Oh, sorry."
  A：「你介意把收音機關小聲一點嗎？」（麻煩你把收音機關小
    聲一點。）
  B：「不，我不介意。」或「一點也不（介意）。」或「當然不
    會（介意）。」或「哦！對不起。」

⑤ Would you mind not **smoking** here？
  麻煩你不要在這邊抽煙好嗎？

（3）表示意願或意圖：

　① I would do it for you.
　　我會為你做這件事。

　② They would fight to the end.
　　他們會奮戰到底。

　③ She wouldn't answer the question.
　　她拒絕回答問題。

（4）表示推測：

　① I thought Lisa would be happy, but not really.
　　我原以為Lisa會很高興，但事實不然。

　② That would be a stolen car.
　　那輛車有可能是贓車。

　　※ would = could = might

（5）表示建議：

　① A: "What should I do?"
　　B: "I would tell her you're sorry."
　　A：我該怎麼辦？
　　B：我會告訴她你很抱歉。

　② I'd go abroad if I were you.
　　如果我是你的話，我會出國。

　　※ I'd = I would，假設語氣 if 用法詳見<u>文法要點</u>。

（6）表示邀請、或提供物品：

【句型】Would you like + $\begin{cases} \text{to + V原形} \\ \text{O} \end{cases}$　你想要…

　① "Would you like to have lunch with me?"
　　= "Do you want to have lunch with me?"
　　"I'd love to." or "I'd like to very much."
　　「能否一起用餐呢？」
　　「我很樂意。」或「榮幸之至。」

　② "Would you like some coffee?"
　　"Yes, please." or "No, thanks."

「要不要來點咖啡？」

「好啊！」或「不用，謝謝。」

③ Would you like a drink?

= Would you care for a drink?

= Care for a drink?（較口語）

要不要來一杯？

（7）表示「要求」的客氣說法：

【句型】**I'd like to + V**　我想要…

　　　　I'd like + O　我想要…

※ like = love，但語氣較弱

① I'd like to try on this T-shirt, please.

我想要試穿這件T恤。

② I'd love to see your new house.

我很想看看你的新房子。

③ I'd like some information about hotels, please?

我想要一些旅館資料。

（8）表示過去的習慣（**=used to**）：

① John would (often) skip class in his school days.

= John used to skip class in his school days.

= John often skipped class in his school days.

John 以前唸書的時候常蹺課。

※ skip class = cut class = cut school = skip school

② My grandmom would (often) tell me many fairy tales when I was a little boy.

我小時候，奶奶常講童話故事給我聽。

（9）用於間接敘述，表示「過去的未來」：

① The weatherman **said** (that) it **would** rain tomorrow.

氣象人員說明天會下雨。

② Judy told me (that) she **wouldn't** come tonight.

Judy 告訴我她今晚不能來。

※ 間接敘述用法詳見文法要點之<u>名詞子句</u>。

玖、WILL

（**1**）表示未來的事件：
　　① I'll be there.
　　　　我會去的。我會出席。我會到。
　　② Will Nina be there tomorrow?
　　　　Nina 明天會去嗎？

（**2**）表示客氣的請求或邀請：
　　① Will you give me a hand?
　　　　= Will you do me a favor?
　　　　= Would you give me a hand?（最客氣）
　　　　= Could you give me a hand?
　　　　= Can you give me a hand?
　　　　你願意幫我嗎？你願助我一臂之力嗎？
　　② Won't you have a seat?
　　　　不坐下來嗎？

（**3**）表示意願、決心或執意：
　　① I'll do my best.
　　　　我會盡力。
　　② She will quit, whatever you say.
　　　　不管你怎麼說，她都要辭職。

（**4**）表示習慣性的動作：
　　① She will often play the piano for hours.
　　　　她鋼琴常常一彈就是好幾個小時。
　　② Tony will play the video games all day.
　　　　= Tony will often play the video games all day.
　　　　= Tony often plays the video games all day.
　　　　Tony 常常一整天打電動。

（5）**won't** 表示拒絕：

① I've asked Kevin for help, but he won't.
我有向 Kevin 求助，但他不肯幫忙。

② The car won't start. What's wrong with it?
這部車發不動，出了什麼毛病？

（6）表示承諾：

① Don't worry. I'll pay you back on Friday.
別擔心，禮拜五我會把錢還給你。

② I won't tell Helen about it, I promise.
我保證不會告訴Helen的。

（7）表示命令，但語氣比 **must** 弱：

① You will pack at once.
你必須馬上打包。

② You'll do as I tell you.
你得照我的命令去做。

（8）其他用法與例句請參考時態之未來式。

拾、SHALL

（1）表示未來的事件，用於第一人稱（I, We）：

　　※ 此屬於英式英語的用法，除了正式書信外，現已漸被 **Will** 所取代。

　　① I shall leave for Hong Kong tomorrow morning.
　　　我將於明天早晨前往香港。

　　② We shall overcome someday.
　　　我們終將得勝。

　　　※ **someday**：將來某一天。

（2）shall we　表示建議

　　① Shall we take a walk?
　　　= Let's take a walk, shall we?
　　　= Shall we go (out) for a walk?
　　　我們去散步，如何？

　　② Shall we go eat?
　　　要不要去吃飯呢？（口語用法）

　　┃ 比　較

　　① Let's do it, shall we?
　　　我們去做，好不好？

　　② Let us do it, will you?
　　　我們去做，你說怎麼樣？

　　③ Let's not do it, OK?
　　　我們不要做，好不好？

（3）shall I　表示徵求對方同意

　　① Shall I move the table (for you)?
　　　= Do you want me to move the table (for you)?
　　　你要我把桌子移開嗎？

　　② Shall I go to the supermarket for you?
　　　你要我去超市幫你買東西嗎？

拾壹、助動詞片語

（1）**had better**　最好是

  ① You (had) better take a rest.

    = You'd better take a rest.

    你最好休息一下。

    ※ 口語常把 **had** 省略。

  ② I'd better be going now.

    = I'd better go now.

    我要走了。

  ③ You'd better not carry too much cash.

    你最好不要帶太多現金。

（2）**ought to**　應該

  （A）表示義務，等於 **should**：

    ① We ought to return these books.

      = We should return these books.

      = We are supposed to return these books.

      我們應該歸還這些書。

    ② You ought to take care of this poor dog.

      你應該照顧這隻可憐的狗。

  （B）表示建議，等於 **should**：

    ① You ought to hang the painting here, not there.

      你應該把畫掛在這裡，而不是那裡。

    ② You ought not to drive too fast.

      = You oughtn't to drive too fast.

      = You shouldn't drive too fast.

      你不應該開得太快。

      ※ **shouldn't** 比 **oughtn't to** 常用。

（3）**had to** 必須（用於過去的事件或行為）

① I had to call the police last night.

我昨晚必須報警。

② The boy was very ill, and I had to take him to the hospital.

當時這個小孩病重，我必須將他送醫治療。

6 動名詞

壹、語法功能

（**1**）作主詞用：

① **Smoking** is bad for health.

抽煙有害健康。

② **Swimming** alone can be dangerous.

一個人游泳有可能發生危險。

③ **Watching baseball games** is exciting.

看球賽很過癮。

（**2**）作受詞用：

① I enjoy **riding a bike**.

我喜歡騎腳踏車。

② Have you finished **writing the letter**?

你信寫完了嗎？

③ We are interested in **collecting stamps**.

我們對集郵有興趣。

（**3**）作補語用：

① Seeing is **believing**.

百聞不如一見。眼見為憑。

② All you have to do is **studying hard**.

= All you have to do is to study hard.

= All you have to is study hard.（較口語，也較常用）

你只要用功就行了。（你所要做的就是努力用功。）

③ My wish is **studying abroad**.

= Studying abroad is my wish.

我的願望就是出國留學。

（4）**not + V-ing** 表示否定

　　① Don't make any excuses for **not wanting** to take the test.
　　　不要找任何藉口說你不想參加考試。

　　② I'm sorry for **not finishing** the project.
　　　很抱歉計畫還沒完成。

（5）**V + being + p.p.** 表示被動

　　① I don't mind **being told** what to do.
　　　我不介意被告知要做什麼。（我不介意別人告訴我要做什麼。）

　　② My brother and I don't enjoy **being laughed at** (by other people).
　　　我跟我弟弟不喜歡被（別人）嘲笑。

貳 、 適 用 情 況

（1）底下的動詞，其後所接的動詞用 **V-ing** 型式：

　　enjoy（喜歡，享受）、finish（完成）、quit（戒除）、consider（考慮）、imagine（想像）、mind（介意）、keep on（繼續）、avoid（避免）、suggest（建議）、appreciate（感激）、practice（練習）、miss（懷念，錯過）、postpone（延後）

　　① I enjoy living in Kaohsiung.
　　　我喜歡住在高雄。

　　② I'll go out when I've finished cleaning the living room.
　　　等我把客廳打掃完畢後就會出門。

　　③ She has quit gambling for three years.
　　　她戒賭已有三年。

④ I'm considering changing my job.
我正在考慮要換工作。

⑤ I don't mind waiting here.
我不介意在這裡等。

⑥ Keep (on) working!
繼續工作！
※ 口語常省略 on

⑦ She tried to avoid answering my question.
她試圖避免回答我的問題。

⑧ I can't imagine living in the Big Apple.
我無法想像在紐約生活的樣子。

⑨ Imagine flunking History!
真想不到我的歷史被當了！

⑩ I would very much appreciate receiving a copy of the book.
如蒙惠贈該書，不勝感激。

⑪ My younger sister usually practices (playing) the piano on Sunday.
我妹妹通常禮拜天練鋼琴。

⑫ Do you miss studying in Canada?
你懷念在加拿大讀書的時光嗎？

⑬ Joe barely missed being hit by a truck.
Joe 差一點被卡車撞了。

⑭ I'll postpone leaving for Australia for a week.
我將延後一個禮拜去澳洲。

⑮ We discussed moving to the countryside.
我們討論搬到鄉下住。

（2）介系詞後的動詞須用 **V-ing**：

① Grandma shows me she's angry by throwing dishes.
Grandma 丟碗盤來向我表示她生氣了。
※ by：藉，以。

② We decided who would wash the dishes **by** flipping a coin.
我們用丟銅板的方式來決定誰去洗碗。

③ I don't blame you **for** lying to me.
我不會怪你對我說謊。

※ **for**：因為。

④ Judy went to work **without** finishing her breakfast.
Judy 沒吃完早餐就去工作。

※ **without**：沒有。

⑤ I **never** see him **without** thinking of his sister.
我每次看到他就想到他妹妹。

※ **never... without**：沒有…而不…，表示雙重否定。

（3）底下常用的片語，因以介系詞結尾，故其後的動詞須用**V-ing**：
be interested in（對…有興趣）、be good at（擅長於）、be fed up with（對…感到厭煩）、be excited about（對…感到興奮）、be fond of（喜歡）、talk about（討論）、be in charge of（負責）、be used to（習慣於）、be capable of（能夠）、be responsible for（負責）、be accused of（被控以…，被責備以…）、complain about/of（抱怨）、insist on（堅持）、look forward to（期盼）、have no excuse for（對…不要找藉口）、prevent...from = stop... (from)（阻止，妨礙）、instead of（取代）、in addition to（除了…之外）

① I'm interested in playing the piano.
我對彈鋼琴有興趣。

② Nina is very good at learning new things.
Nina 擅長學習新事物。

③ This dog is fond of sleeping on the sofa.
這隻狗喜歡睡在沙發上。

④ I'm used to living alone. I don't intend to get married.
我已經習慣一個人住，我不打算結婚。

⑤ Joe insisted on going to the beach with us.
Joe 堅持要跟我們一起去海邊。

⑥　We are looking forward to seeing you soon.

我們盼望能很快地見到你。

※ to 在此為介系詞，而非不定詞。

⑦　He's always complaining about having to work overtime.

他老是抱怨必須要加班。

⑧　You have no excuse for being late.

遲到不要找藉口。

⑨　In addition to working at the bank, James delivers newspapers.

除了在銀行上班之外，James 也送報紙。

※ to 在此為介系詞，而非不定詞。

⑩　The kids were excited about eating at the McDonald's.

孩子們因為能在麥當勞吃東西而感到興奮。

⑪　We talked about going abroad.

我們討論要出國。

（4）**go + V-ing**　表示戶外活動

go shopping（去逛街）、go fishing（去釣魚）、go swimming（去遊泳）、go jogging（去慢跑）、go dancing（去跳舞）、go hiking（去健行）、go hunting（去打獵）、go camping（去露營）、go sailing（去航行）、go skating（去溜冰）、go (mountain) climbing（去爬山）、go skiing（去滑雪）

①　Would you like to go camping with us?

你要不要跟我們去露營？

②　Why don't you go swimming with them?

你何不跟他們一起去游泳呢？

（5）感官動詞，如 **see, hear, feel, find, smell, listen to..., look at** 等，其後之動詞可用 **V-ing** 來表示動作之進行，亦可用 **V** 原形來表示動作之開始到結束。

①　I saw John entering a bar yesterday.

= I saw John enter a bar yesterday.

我昨天看到 John 進入一間酒吧。

② We could hear the rain falling on the roof.

= We could hear the rain fall on the roof.

我們聽到雨落在屋頂上的聲音。

③ I found Jimmy in my room reading my letters.

我發現Jimmy在我房間看我的信。

④ We could smell something burning when we entered the house.

我們進入房子時，聞到有東西燒焦的味道。

⑤ Listen to the cute boy singing!

聽聽這小可愛在唱歌！

⑥ I looked at her painting the sunset.

我看著她畫落日。

（6）**have fun + (in) + V-ing**　玩得愉快

= have a good time + (in) + V-ing

have trouble + (in) + V-ing　有困難

= have difficulty + (in) + V-ing

have a hard/difficult time + (in) + V-ing　很辛苦地，很困難地

① We had fun playing ball.

= We had a good time playing ball.

我們打球打得很開心。

② They had trouble finding their way out.

他們找不到出路。

③ Tim had a hard time dealing with the customer.

Tim 不知如何來應付那位顧客。（即應付得很辛苦。）

④ Did you have any difficulty getting a visa?

你申請簽證有沒有困難？

⑤ I'll have no difficulty passing the road test.

我路考沒有問題。

（7）**spend + 時間 + (in) + V-ing**　花時間於…

　　　waste + 時間 + (in) + V-ing　浪費時間於…

　　① Eric spends most of his time sleeping.

　　　Eric 大部分時間都花在睡覺上面。

　　② Lisa wasted a lot of time daydreaming.

　　　Lisa 浪費很多時間在做白日夢。

　　※ **Judy spent lots of money on clothes.**

　　　Judy 花很多錢在衣服上面。（on＋事物）

（8）**need + V-ing**　需要…（指東西）

　　① The house needs painting.

　　　= The house needs to be painted.

　　　這房子需要油漆。

　　② The car needs fixing.

　　　= The car needs to be fixed.

　　　這車子需要修理。

（9）**be + worth + V-ing**　值得…

　　　be + busy + V-ing　忙於…

　　① The movie is worth seeing twice.

　　　這部電影值得一看再看。

　　② The school is not far at all, so it's not worth taking a taxi.

　　　學校一點也不遠，所以搭計程車不值得／划算。

　　③ The book "War & Peace" is worth reading.

　　　「戰爭與和平」一書值得一讀。

　　④ I'm busy studying for my finals.

　　　我正忙於準備期末考。

（10）**do + some/a lot of/little/a little/any/the... + V-ing**　做…

　　① I'll do some shopping tonight.

　　　我今晚要去買點東西。

② We have to do a lot of reading in high school.
我們高中要唸很多東西。

③ We'll do the cleaning tomorrow morning.
我們明天早上要打掃。

（11）**It's no use/good + V-ing** 做…是無用的
There's no point in + V-ing 做…是沒有意義的

① It's no use talking to the boss.
跟老板說是沒用的。

② It's no good trying to persuade me; I won't change my mind.
想說服我是沒用的，因為我不會改變心意的。

③ There's no point in arguing over this.
為此爭吵沒什麼意義。

7 不定詞

壹、語法功能

（**1**）當主詞：

① **To work with him** is my pleasure.
與他共事是我的榮幸。

② **To speak in public** is not easy.
公開演說並不容易。

③ **To say** is one thing; **to do** is another.
說是一回事，做又是另一回事。

④ **For Tom to love money** is very natural.
Tom 愛錢是很自然的。

（**2**）當受詞：

① We like **to play basketball**.
我們喜歡打籃球。

② I hope **to see you** again soon.
我希望很快再見到你。

③ She promised **to be** here by ten.
她說好十點前到達這裡。

④ Dr. Doty likes **to run** in the afternoon.
Doty 博士喜歡在下午跑步。

（**3**）當補語：

例 ①～③ 為主詞補語，例 ④～⑤ 為受詞補語。

① To see is **to believe**.
= Seeing is believing.
百聞不如一見。

② His ambition is **to be a lawyer**.
他的志向是當一名律師。

③ My hobby is **to collect stamps**.

= My hobby is collecting stamps.

我的嗜好是集郵。

④ I asked him **to stay**.

我要求他留下來。

⑤ You'll find her **to be honest**.

你會發現她很誠實。

※ 當不定詞可以當主詞、受詞和補語時，它便具有名詞的功能，可謂<u>名詞</u><u>不定詞</u>。

（4）當形容詞：

此類不定詞通常置於名詞之後，以修飾名詞。

（A）被修飾的名詞是不定詞的意義主詞：

① The man has no friend **to help him**.

= The man has no friend who will help him.

這位男子沒有朋友可以幫助他。

② You will be the next **to see the manager**.

= You will be the next that will see the manager.

你是下一個去見經理的人。

③ Who was the first **to arrive** last night?

= Who was the first that arrived last night?

昨晚誰先到？

（B）被修飾的名詞是不定詞的意義受詞：

① We have nothing **to do**.

= We have nothing that we can do.

我們沒事可做。

② We've got nothing **to talk about**.

= We've got nothing that we can talk about.

我們沒什麼好談的。

（C）被修飾者若為抽象名詞，則無所謂的意義主詞或受詞：

① I appreciate his ability **to paint**.

我欣賞他繪畫（或油漆）的能力。

② John's father didn't approve of his plan to live abroad.
John 的父親不同意他移居國外的計畫。

③ There's no need to worry.
沒有擔憂的必要。

（5）當副詞：

（A）修飾動詞的不定詞：

① He came to help us.
他來幫我們。（表示目的）

② I've been working day and night to support my family.
= To support my family, I've been working day and night.
我日夜工作為的是要養家活口。

※ to = in order to：為了。

（B）修飾形容詞的不定詞：

① This exercise is easy to do.
= This is an easy exercise to do.
= It is easy to do this exercise.
這個練習很容易做。

② That building is impossible to complete.
= That is an impossible building to complete.
= It is impossible to complete that building.
那幢大樓不可能完成。

③ It is exciting to watch ball games.
= To watch ball games is exciting.
= Watching ball games is exciting.
= It is exciting watching ball games.
看球賽很刺激。

④ You are kind to say so.
= It is kind of you to say so.
= How kind of you to say so!（強調用）
= How kind!
你嘴巴真甜！（此為正面的回應）

⑤ You're nice **to do that.**

= It's nice of you to do that.

= How nice of you to do that!

= How nice!

你真體貼！你真周到！

⑥ I'm afraid **to see my wife cry.**

= I'm afraid of seeing my wife cry.

我很怕看見我太太哭。

⑦ We are surprised **to see you both here.**

= We are surprised at seeing you both here.

真想不到會在這裡見到你們兩位。

⑧ Kevin is likely **to come.**

= Kevin will probably come.

= It is likely that Kevin will come.

Kevin 有可能會來。

⑨ You are really lucky **to pass the test.**

= You're really lucky in passing the test.

你通過考試真是幸運！

⑩ Andy is very slow **to learn English.**

= Andy is very slow in learning English.

Andy 學英文很慢。

⑪ Tim is sure **to need help.**

= Tim will surely need help.

Tim 確實需要幫助。

⑫ The weather is certain **to be fine tomorrow.**

= The weather will certainly be fine tomorrow.

明天天氣一定會放晴。

⑬ I'm ready **to jog.**

= I'm ready for jogging.

我準備好要慢跑了。

（C）修飾副詞的不定詞：

① She is old enough to have a boyfriend.
　她年紀已經夠大，可以交男朋友了。

② The bag is not big enough to hold my toys.
　這個袋子裝不下我的玩具。（即不夠大）

▌比　　較

too... to + V　太…而不能…

too... + not to + V　很…所以不會不…

① Lucy is too young to go to school.
　= Lucy is too young for school.
　= Lucy is too young for going to school.
　Lucy 年紀太小而不能去上學。

② The boss is too smart not to know it.
　= The boss is smart enough to know it.
　老闆很聰明，所以不會不知道這件事。

（6）修飾整句的獨立不定詞：

① To tell the truth, I don't like this idea.
　坦白說，我不喜歡這個構想。

② To begin with, you should follow the rules.
　首先，你必須遵守規則。

③ Strange to say, my roommate didn't come home last night.
　說也奇怪，我室友昨晚沒回來。

（7）**not + to + V**　表示否定

① Please promise (me) not to tell anyone.
　請答應我不要告訴任何人。

② The teacher decided not to give her students a quiz.
　老師決定不給學生小考。

貳、不定詞的形態

V + to + V　簡單不定詞，表示主動，而且其所表達的時間和句子的主要動詞相近。

① She lived to be ninety-four.

= She didn't die until she was ninety-four

她活到九十四歲。

② He will be the first (man) to leave.

= He will be the first (man) that will leave.

他會是第一個離開。

8 被動語態

只有①及物動詞、②不及物動詞加介詞而形成之動詞片語才有被動形式。

【基本句型】**S + be + p.p.（+ by + N）**

（1）現在式之被動式：

　　【句型】**S + am/is/are + p.p.（+ by + N）**

　　① The window is broken.
　　　窗戶壞了。

　　② I'm often invited to parties.
　　　我常被邀請參加派對。

　　③ This room is cleaned every day.
　　　這個房間每天都有人打掃。（字面意思：這個房間每天被打掃。）

　　④ Many car accidents are caused by careless driving.
　　　很多車禍是駕駛疏忽所造成的。

（2）過去式之被動式：

　　【句型】**S + was/were + p.p.（+ by + N）**

　　① This house was built 20 years ago.
　　　這棟房子是二十年前蓋的。

　　② The baby was frightened by the loud noise.
　　　嬰兒被那聲巨響嚇到。

　　③ I was not invited to the wedding.
　　　我沒被邀請參加婚禮。

　　④ They were killed in the car accident.
　　　他們在車禍中喪生。

　　⑤ We were cheated.
　　　我們被騙了。

（3）未來式之被動式：

【句型】（a）S + will/shall + be + p.p.（+ by + N）

（b）S + be going to + be + p.p.（+by + N）

※ 美式英語較少用 shall。

① A new bridge will be built soon.
新橋很快就會建起來。

② A new supermarket is going to be built next month.
新超市將於下個月動工。

③ Two hundred people will be employed by the new company.
新公司將雇用兩百名員工。

④ This room is going to be cleaned later.
這房間待會兒會打掃。

⑤ You'll be killed if he finds you here.
如果他發現你在這裡，你準沒命。

（4）含助動詞之被動式：（表示現在或未來）

【句型】（a）S + must + be + p.p.（+ by + N）
表示肯定的推斷或力勸，意為「一定」、「必須」

（b）S + will + be + p.p.（+ by + N）
表示意志或未來，意為「將要」、「將會」

（c）S + can/could + be + p.p.（+ by + N）
表示能力、推測或允許，意為「能夠」、「可能」、「可以」

（d）S + should + be + p.p.（+ by + N）
表示義務、勸誡或推斷，意為「應該」

（e）S + have/has + to + be + p.p.（+ by + N）
表示力勸，意為「必須」

（f）S + may/might + be + p.p.（+ by + N）
表示推測或允許，意為「可能」、「可以」

（g）S + had better + be + p.p.（+ by + N）
表示建議，意為「最好」

① Something must be done before it's too late.
必須即時採取行動。

② A decision will not be made until the next meeting.
要等到下次會議才做決定。

③ The vase can't be broken.
這個花瓶打不破。

④ This stereo can be carried.
= It's a portable stereo.
這台音響是可以攜帶的。（即手提式音響）

（5）使役式：
使別人為我們做某事或請人服務。
【句型】（a）S + have + O + p.p.
　　　　（b）S + get + O + p.p.（較為急迫）

① I'm going to have my hair cut tomorrow.
我明天要去剪頭髮。

【 比　較 】

I'm going to cut my hair tomorrow.
我明天要自己剪頭髮。

I'm going to **have** John **cut** my hair tomorrow.
= I'll **get** John to **cut my** hair tomorrow.
我明天要叫 John 剪我的頭髮。

② Can I have this photocopied, please?
這文件能否影印一下呢？

③ He's having his car repaired.（強調使別人為我們做某事之事實）
= His car is being repaired.（強調汽車）
他的車子正在送修。

④ Get that car repaired.（語氣較為急迫）
= Have that car repaired.
車子拿去送修。

⑤ We'll get the job done tonight.
我們今晚就會把事情做好。

⑥ Why don't you get that suit cleaned?
你為什麼不把那套西裝送去洗呢？

（6）特殊動詞之被動式：
此類動詞之被動語態與主動語態之意義相同。

① I wasn't prepared to say anything.
= I didn't prepare to say anything.
我不準備發言。

② Judy was graduated from MIT.
= Judy graduated from MIT.（較常用）
Judy 畢業於麻省理工學院。

③ Sue and Rob were married last year.
= Sue and Rob married last year.
= Sue and Rob got married last year.
Sue 和 Rob 於去年結婚。

④ This word is derived from Chinese.
= This word derives from Chinese.
這個字源自中文。

（7）被動慣用語：（表主動意義）

① I'm interested in pop music.
= Pop music interests me.
我對流行音樂感興趣。

② He was surprised at the news.
= The news surprised him.
他對這消息感到驚訝。

③ The boss was not satisfied with my report.
= My report did not satisfy the boss.
老闆不滿意我的報告。

④ The kids **are excited about** the game.

= The game excited the kids.

孩子們對這場比賽感到興奮。

⑤ I **was bored with** the show.

= The show bored me.

= The show was boring to me.

我對這場表演感到無聊。

⑥ The table **is covered with** dust.

這桌子佈滿了灰塵。

⑦ The streets **were crowded with** people.

街上到處是人。

⑧ Her eyes **were filled with** tears.

= Tears filled her eyes.

她的眼睛充滿了淚水。

⑨ He **is known to** everybody around here.

這裡每個人都認識他。

⑩ Judy **is married to** Johnny.

= Johnny is married to Judy.

Judy 嫁給 Johnny。（Johnny 娶 Judy。）

（8）無被動式之動詞：

（A）表示「擁有」的動詞不用被動式，如 have, has。

（B）表示「重量」、「需要」、「尺寸」的動詞不用被動式，如 weigh, take, cost, measure。

（C）表示「發生」的動詞，如 happen, occur, take place。

（D）表示「適合」、「相像」、「使得以維持」之動詞，如 suit, resemble (= take after), last。

① I'm going to have a sports car soon.

我很快就會有部跑車了。

② Tom weighs 200 pounds. That's amazing.

Tom 體重為二百磅。真是嚇人。

③ It took me three hours to finish the job.
這工作花了我三小時才完成。

④ The journey from Taipei to Taichung takes two hours.
從台北到台中的旅程需要兩小時。

⑤ The watch cost two thousand dollars.
這錶價格為兩千元。

⑥ It will cost you $20,000 to fly to Canada.
坐飛機去加拿大要兩萬元。

⑦ What happened last night, Jim?
Jim，昨晚發生什麼事？

⑧ Don't let it happen again.
不要讓它再發生。

⑨ When did the robbery take place?
搶案是什麼時候發生的？

⑩ Our wedding will take place on Sunday.
= Our wedding will be held on Sunday.
我們的婚禮將在禮拜天舉行。

⑪ The sweater suits you well.
這件毛衣很適合你。

（9）以主動語態表示被動意義之動詞：

▌ 特 色

此類動詞雖以主動形式出現，但卻具有被動意義，是故要提醒自己在寫作時，此類動詞不可用被動式，切記。

① The sign says, "No Swimming".
牌子上面寫著：「禁止游泳」。

② This book sells well.
= This is a best-seller.
這是一本暢銷書。

③ Glass breaks easily.
玻璃易碎。

④ The pen writes well.
　這支筆很好寫。

⑤ The shoes don't wear long.
　這雙鞋不耐穿。

⑥ The flower smells good.
　這花聞起來很香。

⑦ The silk feels great.
　這絲織品摸起來很棒。（觸感好）

⑧ (That) sounds great.
　聽起來蠻不錯的。
　※ That 在會話中常省略

⑨ The food tastes delicious.
　這食物嚐起來很美味。

9 比較級

壹、原 級

【句型】（a）**S1 + be + as + adj + as + S2**
（b）**S1 + V + as + adv + as + S2**
S1 和 S2 一樣⋯

① John is as smart as Tom.
John 和 Tom 一樣聰明。

② Mary is as pretty as her older sister.
Mary 和她姐姐一樣漂亮。

③ I can run as quickly as you (can).
我能跑得和你一樣快。

④ He plays tennis as well as Michael.
他網球打得跟 Michael 一樣好。

⑤ Let's walk. It's just as quick as taking the bus.
我們走路好了，反正那跟搭公車一樣快。

※ It 指走路這件事。

【否定句】**not so... as** 沒有某人那麼⋯
not as... as 不像某人那麼⋯

① I'm not so strong as you (are).
我不像你那麼壯。我沒有你壯。

② He can't swim as well as I can/me.
他游泳沒有我行。

※ me 較口語，I can 較合乎文法。

③ Jasmine is not so old as she looks.
Jasmine 的年紀不像她看起來那麼大。（即較「臭老」）

④ He's not so bad as you thought.
他可沒你想的那麼壞。

⑤ Nothing is so precious as life.

沒有什麼東西會跟生命一樣寶貴。（生命是最寶貴的）

= No other thing is more precious than life.

沒有任何其他東西會比生命寶貴。

= Life is more precious than any other thing.

生命比任何其他東西要寶貴。

= Life is the most precious of all.

生命是所有東西當中最寶貴的。

貳、比較級

【句型】（a）**S1 + be + adj-er + than + S2**

（b）**S1 + be + more + adj + than + S2**

（c）**S1 + V + adv-er + than + S2**

（d）**S1 + V + more + adv + than + S2**

S1 比 S2… , S1 比 S2 來得… , S1 比 S2 還要…

┃ 說　明

（1）若形容詞為兩音節以下（如 cold），則用句型（a），　若為三音節（含）以上（如 beautiful），　則用句型（b）。

（2）若副詞為兩音節以下（如 hard），則用句型（c），若為三音節（含）以上，或以 ly 結尾之副詞（如 slowly），則用句型（d）。

（3）若形容詞、副詞為兩音節，則多用第（b）（d）句型，有時則（a）（b）（c）（d）句型並用。若兩音節形容詞的字尾是 y，則其比較級多用去 y 加 ier 的形式，如 busy →busier。

（4）我們拿一個人和另一個人，或一件事物和另一件事物做比較時，則用比較級。

（5）我們拿一個人和另外兩人（含或以上）做比較時，則用最高級，事物比較亦同。

① He's taller than I am.

= He's taller than me.（較口語）

他比我高。

② Linda is more interesting than Cathy.

Linda 比 Cathy 有趣。

③ I work harder than John.

我比 John 賣力。

④ She drives more carefully than you (do).

她開車比你小心。

▌常用形容詞之比較級

（1）字尾加 **er**：

　　① clean（乾淨的）→ cleaner

　　② cold（冷的）→ colder

　　③ cheap（便宜的）→ cheaper

　　④ old（老的）→ older

　　⑤ young（年輕的）→ younger

　　⑥ near（近的）→ nearer

　　⑦ light（輕的）→ lighter

　　⑧ warm（暖的）→ warmer

　　⑨ cool（涼的，酷的）→ cooler

　　⑩ tall（高的）→ taller

　　⑪ short（矮的，短的）→ shorter

　　⑫ long（長的）→ longer

　　⑬ strong（壯的）→ stronger

　　⑭ weak（弱的）→ weaker

（2）字尾加 **r**：

　　① nice（好的）→ nicer

　　② large（大的）→ larger

③ fine（好的，晴朗的）→ finer
④ safe（安全的）→ safer
⑤ wise（明智的）→ wiser
⑥ wide（寬的）→ wider
⑦ late（晚的，新近的）→ later

（3）重覆字尾加 **er**：
① big（大的）→ bigger
② hot（熱的，熱門的）→ hotter
③ fat（胖的）→ fatter
④ wet（濕的）→ wetter
⑤ sad（悲傷的）→ sadder
⑥ thin（瘦的，薄的）→ thinner

（4）去 **y** 加 **ier**：
① dry（乾的）→ drier
② pretty（美麗的）→ prettier
③ friendly（友善的）→ friendlier
④ tidy（整齊的）→ tidier
⑤ busy（忙碌的）→ busier
⑥ funny（好笑的）→ funnier
⑦ merry（快樂的）→ merrier
⑧ crazy（瘋狂的）→ crazier
⑨ early（早的）→ earlier
⑩ heavy（重的）→ heavier

（5）字尾加 **er** 或前面加 **more**：
① clever（聰明的）→ cleverer/more clever
② quiet（安靜的）→ quieter/more quiet
③ simple（簡單的，單純的）→ simpler/more simple
④ narrow（窄的）→ narrower/more narrow

⑤ stupid（笨的）→ stupider/more stupid

⑥ happy（快樂的）→ happier/more happy

（6）前面加 **more**：

① correct（正確的）→ more correct

② famous（有名的）→ more famous

③ careful（小心的）→ more careful

④ careless（粗心的）→ more careless

⑤ interesting（有趣的）→ more interesting

⑥ beautiful（美麗的）→ more beautiful

⑦ wonderful（美妙的，極佳的）→ more wonderful

⑧ expensive（昂貴的）→ more expensive

⑨ important（重要的）→ more important

※ often（經常）→ **more often**

slowly（慢地）→ **more slowly**

seriously（嚴重地，正經地）→ **more seriously**

任何以 **ly** 結尾之副詞，其比較級形式皆為 **more + adv**。

不規則比較級

（1）many/much（多的）→ more

（2）little（少的）→ less（用於不可數名詞）

few（少的）→ fewer（用於可數名詞）

（3）good/well（好的）→ better

（4）bad/ill（壞的）→ worse

（5）well-off（富有的）→ better-off

（6）badly-off（窮的）→ worse-off

（7）well-to-do（有錢的）→ better-to-do

（8）far（遠的）→ farther/further（更進一步的）

（9）well-known（著名的）→ better-known

（10）badly（壞地）→ worse

① My room is cleaner than yours.
我的房間比你的乾淨。

② This watch is cheaper than that one.
這隻手錶比那隻便宜。

③ That shirt looks nicer than this one.
那件襯衫看起來比這件好看。

④ I won't marry anyone fatter than you.
= I won't marry anyone who is fatter than you.
我不會娶／嫁比你胖的人。

⑤ I feel sadder than you (do).
我比你感到更悲傷。

⑥ Your desk is tidier than hers.
你的書桌比她的要來得整齊。

⑦ Your joke is funnier than mine.
你的笑話比我的好笑。

⑧ She's cleverer than you.
= She's more clever than you.
她比你聰明。

⑨ Kids are simpler than adults.
= Kids are more simple than adults.
小孩比大人來得單純。

⑩ You're more careful than your brother (is) in choosing friends.
你在擇友方面比你兄弟謹慎。

⑪ In my opinion, Michael Jordan is more famous than Michael Jackson.
以我之見，Michael Jordan（籃球明星）比 Michael Jackson（樂壇巨人）有名。

⑫ Her story is more interesting than John's.
她的故事比 John 的有趣。

⑬ You must have more money than I do.
你的錢一定比我多。
※ **more** 在此為形容詞比較級。

⑭ You exercise more often than I do.

你比我常運動。

※ **more** 在此為副詞比較級。

⑮ I'm better at English than Jim, but worse at math.

我英文比 Jim 好，但數學比他差。

※ **better** 和 **worse** 在此為形容詞比較級。

⑯ Nobody plays basketball better than you (do).

沒有人籃球打得比你好。

※ **better**在此為副詞比較級。

⑰ You eat less than I do.

你吃得比我少。

※ **less** 在此為副詞比較級。

▌ 否定比較級

【句型】 **S1 + be + not +** 形容詞比較級 **+ than + S2**

　　　　 S1 不比 **S2** 更…

　　　　 S1 + be + less + adj（三音節以上）**+ than + S2**

　　　　 S1 比 **S2** 更不…

① I'm not taller than **her/she is.**

= I'm shorter than her/she is.

= She's taller than me/I am.

我不比她高。（她比我高）

※ 口語用 **her, me**，正式用 **she is, I am**。

② Judy is **more** beautiful **than** Jenny.

= Jenny is **less** beautiful **than** Judy.

= Judy is prettier than Jenny.

= Jenny is uglier than Judy.

Judy 比 Jenny 漂亮。（Jenny 比 Judy 醜）

省略式比較級

若比較的事物明確的話，則可省略 **than** 及名詞。

① John plays the piano very well, but I play better.
John 鋼琴彈得很好，不過我彈得更好。

② I'm trying to exercise more and eat less.
我試圖多運動少吃東西。

③ You'll have to be more careful next time.
你以後必須更小心。

④ It's cold in London, but it's colder here.
倫敦很冷，但這裡更冷。

⑤ Please help me more with the housework, OK?
請幫忙多做點家事，好嗎？

⑥ He's bad at Mandarin, but I'm worse.
他國語不好，而我則更差。

⑦ I'm good at sports, but she's better.
我擅長運動，不過她更行。

⑧ Can you speak more slowly?
請你說話慢一點好嗎？

⑨ I don't play basketball a lot these days. I used to play more often.
我最近不常打籃球，以前比較常打。

⑩ She has never been happier (than she is now).
她不曾如此快樂過。（現在她感到最快樂）

比較級注意事項

（1）比較級前面可以接 **much**（但不可接 **many**）、**a lot**（＝ **much**）、**far** 來加強語氣：

① Let's go by bus. It's much cheaper.
我們坐公車去，那便宜多了。

② Your sweater is a lot more expensive than mine.
你的毛衣比我的貴很多。

③ The situation was far more serious than I expected.
情況比我預期的要嚴重許多。

（2）比較級前面可以接 any, not, no：
① Do you feel any better today?
你今天有沒有好一點？
② I'm not waiting any longer.
= I'm not waiting any more.
我不要再等下去。
※ any more = anymore

（3）比較級前面也可以接 a little（有一點）、a bit（= a little）、
a little bit（有一點）來表示程度上略勝一籌：
① Can't you stay a little longer?
你不能多待一會兒嗎？
② Could you speak a bit more slowly?
能不能說話慢一點？

（4）比較級後面不用 than 而出現 of the two 時，比較級前面須加
定冠詞 the：
① Jenny is the younger of the two (girls).
Jenny 是兩個女孩當中較年輕的那一位。
② Michael is the taller of the twins.
Michael 是雙胞胎裡面較高的。

（5）比較的對象一定要相當：
① The climate of Kaohsiung is hotter than that of Taipei.
高雄的氣候比台北熱。
② The pleasure of singing is greater than that of dancing.
唱歌的樂趣大於跳舞。

比較級常用句型

（1）比較級 **+ and +** 比較級　愈來愈…

① It is becoming **harder and harder** to find a good job nowadays.
現今要找份好工作是愈來愈難了。

② Your English is getting **better and better**.
你的英文愈來愈好了。

③ It's growing **more and more difficult** to survive in big cities.
要在大城市生存是愈來愈難了。

※ **grow = get = become**：變得。

④ There are **more and more** people learning computers.
= **More and more** people are learning computers.
愈來愈多的人在學電腦。

⑤ The balloon went up **higher and higher** in the air.
氣球在空中愈飛愈高。

（2）**The +** 比較級**, the +** 比較級　愈…愈…

① The more, the better.
愈多愈好。（多多益善）

② The sooner, the better.
愈快愈好。

③ **The less** baggage you carry, **the better**.
你帶的行李愈少愈好。

④ **The older** one grows, **the poorer** his memory becomes.
一個人年紀愈大，記性就愈差。

⑤ **The younger** you are, **the easier** it is to learn English.
年紀愈小，學英語愈容易。

⑥ **The more** I look at this painting, **the better** I like it.
這幅畫我愈看愈喜歡。（我愈看這幅畫，就愈喜歡它。）

另類比較級

此類比較級雖沒有一般比較級之形式（如 **more... than**）但卻具有比較級之意義。

【句型1】 **S + prefer + A + to + B**

　　　　　 喜歡⋯甚於⋯，寧願⋯也不願，與其⋯不如⋯

① I prefer tea to coffee.
　 我喜歡茶勝於咖啡。

② I prefer dying to working there.
　 我寧願死也不願在那裡工作。

【句型2】 **S1 + be + different from + S2**　 與⋯不同
　　　　　 S1 + be + similar to + S2　 與⋯類似

① My new computer is different from my old one.
　 我的新電腦跟舊的不一樣。

② Her hairstyle is similar to mine.
　 她的髮型跟我的類似。

參、最高級

【句型】（a）S + be + the + adj-est（+ N/of all/in the...）

（b）S + be + the + most + adj（+ N/of all/in the...）

（c）S + V + the + adv-est（+ N/of all/in the...）

（d）S + V + the + most + adv（+ N/of all/in the...）

某人／物最…，某人／物…最…

說　明

（1）若形容詞為單音節（如 clean），則用（a）、（c）句型。

（2）若形容詞為三音節（含）以上（如 interesting），則用（b）、（d）句型。

（3）若形容詞為兩音節（如 modern），則多用（b）句型，有時亦可用（a）句型（如 simple）。

（4）以 y 為結尾的形容詞，用（a）句型，但其最高級變為：去 y 加 iest，如 busy → busiest。

（5）若副詞為單音節（如 fast），則用第（c）句型。

（6）若副詞為三音節（含）以上（如 carefully），則用第（d）句型。

（7）若副詞以 ly 結尾，則不管多少音節，一律用（d）句型。

（8）最高級與比較級的形式可相互參照，如 cleaner → the cleanest；more careful → the most careful。

① Peter is the tallest of all.

　 Peter 是裡頭最高的。

② This is the most correct statement.

　 這個是最正確的敘述。

③ Jenny seems (to be) the most clever of the three girls.

　 = Jenny seems (to be) the cleverest of the three girls.

　 Jenny 似乎是三個女孩當中最聰明的。

④ This one is the most expensive of all.

　 這個是裡頭最貴的。

⑤ It's the most boring book I've ever read.

　 這是我看過最無聊的書。

⑥ Jim worked the hardest in the company.

　 Jim 在公司最勤奮。

⑦ He ran the most quickly of all.
他跑得最快。

⑧ Which is the longest river in the world?
全球最長的河流是哪一條？

▌常用形容詞之最高級

（1）字尾加 est：

① clean（乾淨的）→ cleanest
② clear（清楚的）→ clearest
③ cold（冷的）→ coldest
④ warm（溫暖的）→ warmest
⑤ cool（涼的，棒的）→ coolest
⑥ mild（溫和的）→ mildest
⑦ cheap（便宜的）→ cheapest
⑧ old（老的）→ oldest
⑨ young（年輕的）→ youngest
⑩ near（近的）→ nearest
⑪ light（輕的）→ lightest
⑫ tall（高的）→ tallest
⑬ short（矮的，短的）→ shortest
⑭ strong（強壯的）→ strongest
⑮ weak（弱的）→ weakest
⑯ great（偉大的）→ greatest

（2）字尾加 st：

① nice（美好的）→ nicest
② large（大的）→ largest
③ fine（好的，晴朗的）→ finest
④ safe（安全的）→ safest
⑤ wise（明智的）→ wisest
⑥ wide（寬的）→ widest
⑦ late（新近的，晚的）→ latest
⑧ cute（可愛的）→ cutest

（3）重覆字尾加 **est**：
　　① big（大的）→ biggest
　　② hot（熱的，熱門的）→ hottest
　　③ fat（胖的）→ fattest
　　④ wet（濕的）→ wettest
　　⑤ sad（悲傷的）→ saddest
　　⑥ thin（瘦的，薄的）→ thinnest

（4）去 **y** 加 **iest**：
　　① dry（乾的）→ driest
　　② pretty（漂亮的）→ prettiest
　　③ friendly（友善的）→ friendliest
　　④ tidy（整齊的）→ tidiest
　　⑤ busy（忙碌的）→ busiest
　　⑥ funny（好笑的）→ funniest
　　⑦ merry（快樂的）→ merriest
　　⑧ crazy（瘋狂的）→ craziest
　　⑨ early（早的）→ earliest
　　⑩ heavy（重的）→ heaviest

（5）字尾加 **est** 或前面加 **most**：
　　① clever（聰明的）→ cleverest/most clever
　　② common（普通的）→ commonest/most common
　　③ quiet（安靜的）→ quietest/most quiet
　　④ simple（簡單的）→ simplest/most simple
　　⑤ narrow（窄的）→ narrowest/most narrow
　　⑥ stupid（笨的）→ stupidest/most stupid
　　⑦ happy（快樂的）→ happiest/most happy

（6）前面加 **most**：
　　① correct（正確的）→ most correct
　　② famous（有名的）→ most famous
　　③ careful（小心的）→ most careful

④ careless（粗心的）→ most careless
⑤ interesting（有趣的）→ most interesting
⑥ beautiful（美麗的）→ most beautiful
⑦ wonderful（美妙的，極佳的）→ most wonderful
⑧ intelligent（聰明的）→ most intelligent
⑨ expensive（昂貴的）→ most expensive
⑩ important（重要的）→ most important
⑪ often（經常）→ most often
⑫ serious（嚴重的）→ most serious

不規則最高級

（1）good（好的）→ best
（2）well（好的）→ best
（3）wrong（錯的）→ worst
（4）ill（壞的）→ worst
（5）many/much（多的）→ most
（6）little/few（少的）→ least
（7）far（遠的）→ farthest/furthest
（8）late（遲的，新近的）→ latest（最遲的／最近的），last（最後的）
① It's the latest design.
　 這是最新的設計款式。
② That's the worst thing I've ever seen.
　 那是我見過最糟的東西。

最高級注意事項

（1）三個以上的人或物相比，須用最高級；兩個相比則用比較級：
① Tom is the smartest student in my class.
　 Tom 是我班上最聰明的學生。
② Judy is the most diligent of the (three) girls.
　 Judy 是（三人）當中最勤奮的。

③ I like spring (the) best of all the seasons.
四季中我最喜歡春天。
※ of all the seasons 可省略。

④ I like winter better/more than summer.
我喜歡冬天勝過夏天。

（2）**the least + adj**　最不⋯
　　the most + adj　最⋯

① This one is the least expensive of all.
這個是裡面最不貴的。（即最便宜的）

② That is the most expensive watch of the three.
那隻錶是三隻裡面最貴的。

③ Your joke is the least interesting of all.
你的笑話是最不好笑的。

（3）**the last**　最後的，最不可能的
　　the latest　最新的，最近的，最遲的

① He was the last man to leave.
= He was the last man that left.
他是最後才離開的。

② As your best friend, Tom is the last man to cheat you.
身為你最好的朋友，Tom 是最不可能會欺騙你的。

③ This is the latest design I can get.
這是我所能拿到最新的款式。

④ He came the latest of all.
他最晚來。

（4）最高級代換句型：（初中高級適用）

① Time is the most precious of all.
= Nothing is so precious as time.
= Time is more precious than any other thing.
= No other thing is more precious than time.
= No other thing is so/as precious as time.
時間是一切東西中最寶貴的。

② Taipei is the biggest city in Taiwan.

= No other city in Taiwan is bigger than Taipei.

= Taipei is bigger than any other city in Taiwan.

= Taipei is bigger than all the other cities in Taiwan.

= No other city in Taiwan is so big as Taipei.

= Taipei is the biggest of all the cities in Taiwan.

= Taipei is as big as any city in Taiwan.

台北是台灣最大的城市。

③ John is the best speaker of English in our community.

= No one speaks English so well as John (does).

John 是我們社區英語講得最好的人。

④ "Titanic" is the most touching movie I have ever seen.

= I have never seen a movie more touching than "Titanic".

「鐵達尼號」是我看過最感人的電影。

⑤ We arrived here earliest of the guests.

= No other guest arrived here earlier than we did/us.

我們是最早到的。

（5）若不與其他人事物作比較，則 **most = very**，且其前不加 **the**，
而用 **a** 或 **an**：

① She was a most brave woman.

她是一個很勇敢的女性。

② This is a most funny book.

這是一本很有趣的書。

（6）最高級若出現在句首，則常會有 even（甚至）的意味：

① The smartest boy in the class could not answer the question.

即使是班上最聰明的學生也不會回答這個問題。

② The largest sum of money cannot buy health.

即使再多的錢也買不到健康。

10 分詞

分詞構句屬於中高級以上程度，所以在此略去。

壹、現在分詞 V-ing

（1）表主動或進行狀態：
① There are a lot of boys **playing** in the garden.
有很多男孩在花園裡玩耍。
② A **drowning** man will catch at a straw.
溺水的人連一根稻草也要抓。（急不暇擇）

（2）表性質：
① That's a very **disappointing** action.
那是一項令人失望的舉動。
② That **tiring** job really killed me.
那累人的工作真要我的命。

（3）表主詞補語：
① The girl came **crying** to her mother.
那女孩哭著走向她媽媽。
② The man ran **shouting** on the street.
那個男的在街上邊跑邊叫。

（4）表受詞補語：
① The joke set all the students **laughing**.
這個笑話使全班哄堂大笑。

② Did you find him **waiting** for you?
你有沒有發現他在等你？

（5）表副詞：
① It's **boiling** hot today.
今天天氣熱死了。
② It's **freezing** cold, isn't it?
= It's **freezing**, isn't it?
好冷，不是嗎？

貳、過去分詞 V-ed

（1）表被動：
① **Stolen** fruit tastes sweet.
偷來的水果是甜的。
② This grocery store sells a lot of **frozen** food.
這家雜貨店賣很多冷凍食品。

（2）表情緒或心態：
① I'm **interested** in pop music.
我對流行音樂有興趣。
② His boss was not **satisfied** with his report.
他老闆不滿意他的報告。

（3）表主詞補語：
① The dog was found **killed** on the sidewalk.
這隻狗被發現死於人行道上。

② I came home very tired last night.
我昨晚回家時累歪了。

（4）表受詞補語：

① I found the man hurt on the street.
我在街上發現這個人受傷了。

② Lisa could not make herself understood in English.
Lisa 無法用英語表達自己的意思。

11 假設語氣

壹、與現在事實相反之假設法

【句型】If + S + $\begin{cases} \text{p.t.（動詞過去式）} \\ \text{were} \end{cases}$, S + $\begin{cases} \text{would} \\ \text{could} \\ \text{might} \\ \text{should} \end{cases}$ + V原形

① If I had enough money, I would buy a motorbike.
　假如我現在有足夠的錢，我會去買摩托車。

② If I knew how to swim, I would go to the beach with you.
　假如我會游泳，我會跟你去海灘。

③ If May had time, she would go to the movies with you.
　假如 May 有空的話，她會陪你去看電影。

④ If the weather were nice, I would go jogging.
　假如天氣不錯的話，我會去慢跑。

⑤ If Tim were here, he would kill you.
　假如 Tim 人在這裡，他會宰了你。

⑥ If I were you, I wouldn't lend him money.
　假如我是你，我不會把錢借給他。

貳、與過去事實相反之假設法

【句型】If + S + had p.p., S + $\begin{cases} \text{would} \\ \text{could} \\ \text{might} \\ \text{should} \end{cases}$ + have p.p.

① If I had had enough money, I would have bought a car.
假如當時我有足夠的錢,那我會去買部車子。

② If Jenny had worked hard, she would have passed the test.
假如 Jenny 那時候用功的話,那她早就通過考試了。

③ If the weather had been nice, we might have climbed Mt. Ali.
假如當時天氣好的話,我們可能會去爬阿里山。

④ If she had obeyed the doctor's directions, she wouldn't have died.
假如她當時聽從醫師的話,她就不會死了。

⑤ If you had not helped me, I would have failed.
假如你那時候沒有幫我,我就會失敗。

參、與未來事實相反之假設法

【句型】

（a）If + S + should + V原形, S + $\begin{cases} \text{would} \\ \text{could} \\ \text{might} \\ \text{should} \end{cases}$ 或 $\begin{cases} \text{will} \\ \text{can} \\ \text{may} \\ \text{shall} \end{cases}$ + V原形

（b）**If +S + were to + V原形, S +** $\left\{\begin{array}{l}\textbf{would}\\\textbf{could}\\\textbf{might}\\\textbf{should}\end{array}\right.$ **+ V原形**

① If Kent should fail, he would be very sad.
  萬一 Kent 失敗了，他會很傷心。

② If Mary should pass the test, her parents would be very happy.
  萬一 Mary 通過考試，她父母會很高興的。

③ If the sun were to rise in the west, I would buy you dinner.
  如果太陽打從西邊出來，那我就請你吃飯。

④ If you were to be reborn, what would you do ?
  如果你去投胎的話，你要做什麼？

肆、可能發生之假設法

【句型】**If + S + V, S +** $\left\{\begin{array}{l}\textbf{will}\\\textbf{can}\\\textbf{may}\\\textbf{shall}\end{array}\right.$ **+ V原形**

① If you need some money, I can lend you some.
  如果你需要點錢，我可以借你一些。

② If it is fine tomorrow, I will go hiking.
  如果明天天氣晴朗的話，我會去健行。

③ If the news is true, my father will be glad.
  如果消息正確的話，我父親會高興。

伍、WISH 但願，要是…就好了

（**1**）與現在事實相反：

【句型】S1 + wish (that) + $\begin{Bmatrix} \text{S1} \\ \text{S2} \end{Bmatrix}$ + $\begin{Bmatrix} \text{p.t.（動詞過去式）} \\ \text{were} \end{Bmatrix}$

※ 若為普通動詞，則用過去式；若為 be 動詞，則用 were。

① I wish I knew how to swim.
　但願我會游泳。

② I wish I had a sports car.
　要是我有一部跑車就好了。

③ Judy wishes she didn't have to work this afternoon.
　Judy 好希望她今天下午不用上班。

④ Mike wishes his girlfriend would marry him.
　Mike 真希望他的女朋友願意嫁給他。

⑤ I wish it were cooler today.
　今天天氣若涼一點，那該有多好！

⑥ Anne wishes she were in Paris.
　Anne 好希望她現在人在巴黎。

（**2**）與過去事實相反：

【句型】S1 + $\begin{Bmatrix} \text{wish (that)} \\ \text{wished (that)} \end{Bmatrix}$ + $\begin{Bmatrix} \text{S1} \\ \text{S2} \end{Bmatrix}$ + had p.p.

① I wish (that) I had studied for the test.
　但願我那時候有好好準備考試。

② Jacky wishes he had visited his uncle.
　Jacky 好希望那時候他有去找他叔叔。

③ I wish I hadn't gone to the movies.
　但願那時沒去看那部電影。
　（但不幸卻去看了，所以現在後悔不已。）

④ I wish I had had enough money.
　但願那時我有足夠的錢。（那麼我就可以…）

⑤ We wish the weather had been nice.
我們好希望當時天氣晴朗。

⑥ I wish I had been to New York.
但願我曾去過紐約。

12 子句

【說明】

　　子句就是句子裡的句子；亦即一個長句子可以切成兩個
（含）以上的簡單句（simple sentence）或短句子（符合
五大基本句型的句子），那這幾個句子便稱為子句。

《分類》

（1）對等子句：由對等連接詞（如 and, or, but, either...
　　 or..., neither... nor..., not... but...）所連接的兩
　　 個（含）以上之獨立子句，稱為對等子句。此類子
　　 句位階相等，沒有主從之分，且在結構上與內容上必
　　 須對稱。

（2）獨立子句與附屬子句：由附屬連接詞（如 when, if,
　　 because, as, though）所連接的兩個子句，其一可
　　 獨立存在，稱為獨立子句或主要子句；另一必須依附
　　 獨立子句，稱為附屬子句或次要子句。換句話說，由
　　 附屬連接詞所引導的句子稱為附屬子句，而沒有附屬
　　 連接詞所引導的句子稱為獨立子句。從語法的功能來
　　 說，附屬子句是用來修飾獨立子句的，亦即獨立子
　　 句是紅花，而附屬子句是綠葉，所以有「主從」之分。
　　 例如：I didn't go to school because I was sick.
　　 獨立子句：I didn't go to school.（可獨立存在）
　　 附屬子句：I was sick.（不可獨立存在，其中 because
　　 　　　　　 為附屬連接詞）
　　 附屬子句依語法功能又可區分為①副詞子句、②名詞
　　 子句、③形容詞子句或關係子句。

壹、對等子句

【句型1】 **S + V, and + S + V** …而且…

S + V, or + S + V …或者…

① We got married two years ago, **and** we had a boy last year.

我們兩年前結婚，去年生了一個男孩。

② You may pay cash, **or** you may use a credit card.

你可以付現或者刷卡。

補　充

and, or, but 除了可以連接對等子句外，也可連接對等詞語（如動詞、名詞、形容詞、副詞…）。此外，or 亦可作「否則」解。

① I'll stay home **and** watch TV tonight.

我今晚要待在家裡看電視。

② I'll treat you **and** your family well.

我會善待你和你的家人。

③ Would you like coffee **or** tea?

你要咖啡還是茶？

④ Hurry up, **or** you'll be late.

快一點，否則你會遲到。

⑤ She's pretty **and** smart.

= She's **both** pretty **and** smart.

= She's **not only** pretty **but (also)** smart.

她漂亮又聰明。

※ **not only... but (also)...**：不但…而且…；**both... and...**：兩者兼具。此亦屬於對等連接詞，可連接對等子句或詞語。

【句型2】**either... or...** 不是…就是…，可以…也可以…

① **Either** I pick you up at 6 **or** you go yourself.
不是我六點來接你，就是你自己去。

② **Either** you can take the final exam **or** you can write a term paper.
= You can either take the final exam or write a term paper.
你可以參加期末考，也可以寫期末報告。

補　充

either... or... 除了可連接對等子句外，亦可連接對等詞語（如名詞、形容詞…）。

① We may go there **either** on foot **or** by bus.
我們可以走路去，也可以搭公車。

② **Either** she **or** I **am** responsible for this.
不是她就是我要對這件事負責。

比　較

neither... nor... 不是…也不是…（後接對等詞語）

① He can **neither** sing **nor** dance.
他不會唱歌也不會跳舞。

② **Neither** John nor Mary **knows** it.
John 和 Mary 都不知道這件事。

③ She cannot type, nor/neither can she speak English.
她不會打字，也不會說英語。

④ He **neither** did his homework, **nor** did he feel sorry for it.
他沒有寫功課，也沒有為此感到抱歉。

【句型3】 S + V, but/yet + S + V ···雖然···但是···（表反義）

① He's rich, **but** he's not happy.
　　他雖有錢，但並不快樂。

② You promised, **yet** you've done nothing.
　　你答應了，可是你卻什麼也沒做。

｜ 補　充

but, yet 除了可連接對等子句外，亦可連接對等詞語。但 yet 的語氣較緩和。

① Mr. Johnson is old but strong.
　　Johnson 先生人雖老邁但身體硬朗。

② That is strange yet true.
　　那雖奇怪，但卻是千真萬確的。

貳、修飾獨立子句之附屬子句

（1）副詞子句

功能 1

表時間之附屬連接詞，如 when, while, as, before, after, until（直到）, as soon as（一…就…）所引導之副詞子句。

① I used to cry a lot **when** I was a little boy.

= **When** I was a little boy, I used to cry a lot.

我小時候很愛哭。

　　※ **used to + V**：表示過去的習慣或事實。

② I did**n't** go to bed **until** Mother turned off the TV.

直到媽媽把電視關掉，我才去睡覺。

③ I haven't heard from him **since** he went to Canada.

自從他去加拿大，我就一直沒有他的消息。

I haven't seen her **since** 1990.

自從一九九〇年以來，我就再也沒有看到她。

　　※ since（自從）的句型：

　　　　S + have/has + p.p. + since + S + V過去式

　　　　S + have/has + p.p. + since + 過去時間

④ I'll phone you **as soon as** I get there.

= **As soon as** I get there, I'll phone you.

我一到那裡，我就打電話給你。

⑤ I lost my wallet **while** (I was) taking a walk in the park.

= **While** (I was) taking a walk in the park, I lost my wallet.

當我在公園散步時，我掉了皮夾。

功能 2

表原因之附屬連接詞（如 because）所引導之副詞子句。

I didn't go to school because I was sick.

= Because I was sick, I didn't go to school.

= I was sick, so I didn't go to school.

= I was sick; therefore, I didn't go to school.

我因為生病所以沒去學校。

※ **therefore**：因此。為連接性副詞，用來連接兩個句子。

功能 3

表條件之附屬連接詞（如 if）所引導之副詞子句。

① The game will be canceled if it snows.

= If it snows, the game will be canceled.

如果下雪，比賽就得取消。

② If you are good at English, you'll have more job opportunities.

如果你英文好的話，你會有更多的工作機會。

※ 假設語氣的用法，在中高級會詳述，初級英檢一般只考「可能
發生之假設法」，即此例句之用法。

功能 4

表讓步之附屬連接詞，如 though/although, whether...or not（不
論…與否）所引導之副詞子句。

① I'm happy although I'm poor.

= I'm happy though poor.

= I'm poor, but I'm happy.

= Although I'm poor, I'm happy.

我雖然窮，但很快樂。

※ **although** 和 **but** 不可並用。

② Whether it may rain or shine, we'll go on a picnic on Sunday.

無論晴雨，我們禮拜天都要去野餐。

功能 5

表結果之附屬連接詞，如 so that, so...that..., such that, such...
that...（如此…以致於…）所引導之副詞子句。

The kid was **so** clever **that** he solved the problem quickly.

= The kid was clever **enough to** solve the problem quickly.

這小孩很聰明，所以很快就把問題解決了。

功能 6

表做法之附屬連接詞，如 as（照著）所引導之副詞子句。

① Do **as** I tell you.

　= Do **as** I say.

　照我說的去做。

② You should play basketball **as** the coach shows you.

　你應該按照教練的示範動作來打籃球。

③ When in Rome, do **as** the Romans do.

　入境隨俗。

④ Take life **as** it is.

　接受人生的原貌。（順應天命）

（**2**）名詞子句：

說　明

附屬子句若拿來當名詞用，而在語法結構上形成具有主詞、受詞或補語功用的附屬子句，則稱為名詞子句。

（A）由 that 所引導的名詞子句：

使用時機

當我們要將一個敘述句（S + V）降格成一個名詞時。

【句型1】S + V + (that) + S + V

※ **that** 可省略，尤其在會話上。

① I believe (that) Jane is a good girl.

　我們相信 Jane 是個好女孩。

② We think (that) Jim does well in school.

　我們認為 Jim 在學校的表現很好。

③ He thought (that) he was not wrong.

　他認為他沒有錯。

【句型2】S + V + O + that + S + V

① He told me that he was fired.

他告訴我他被炒魷魚。

② I advised her that she should wait patiently.

= I advised her to wait patiently.

我建議她要耐心等候。

【句型3】It is adj/N + that + S + V

　　　　　That + S + V + is + adj/N

① It is true that he is a nice guy.

= That he is a nice guy is true.（that 不可省略）

他人很好是真的。

② It was a fact that James wanted to marry an American woman.

= That James wanted to marry an American woman was a fact.（that 不可省略）

James 要娶美國太太是一項事實。

【句型4】S + be + adj/p.p. + that + S + V

① I'm glad that you could come.

= I'm glad of your coming.

我很高興你能來。

② I'm sorry that I'm late.

= I'm sorry to be late.

= I'm sorry for being late.

很抱歉遲到了。

③ She was not aware that there was a difficulty.

= She was not aware of the difficulty.

她不知道有困難。

（B）由 whether 或 if 所引導之名詞子句：

使用時機

當我們要將一個 yes/no question 降格成一個名詞使用時。

【句型1】 S + V + whether (or not) + S + V

　　　　　 S + V + whether + S + V + (or not)

① She asked me whether I was angry.

= She asked me whether or not I was angry.

= She asked me whether I was angry or not.

她問我是不是生氣了。

② We want to know whether you have fixed the car.

我們想知道你是否已修好車子。

【句型2】 S + V + if + S + V

① I don't know if she's from Japan.

我不知道她是不是來自日本。

② I wonder if you could help me.

不曉得你能不能幫個忙。

③ I'll see if I can read it.

我看看是否能解讀這個東西。

（C）由疑問詞所引導之名詞子句：

使用時機

當我們要將一個由 what, where, who, how, when, why 等疑問詞開頭的疑問句降格成一個名詞使用時。

【句型】 S + V（+ O）+ 疑問詞 + S + V

① She asked (me) where I was going.（間接問句）

= She said (to me),"Where are you going?"（直接問句）

她問我要去哪裡？

② Tom asked (me) who that woman was.（間接問句）

= Tom asked (me),"Who is that woman?"（直接問句）

Tom 問我那個女的是誰。

※ 由疑問句如**what**等所引導之名詞子句，其主詞與動詞的位置須用<u>常態順序</u>（即 **S + V**，不須倒裝），而疑問詞則當連接詞用。

※ 由直接問句轉為間接問句，不僅引號內的人稱須做調整，而且時態亦須降一格，亦即引號內若為現在式，則改為過去式。同理，現在進行式 → 過去進行式，現在未來式 → 過去未來式（即 **will → would；can't → couldn't**等）。

③ Nobody believes what she says.
沒人相信他的話。

④ I know how you feel.
我了解你的感受。

⑤ Can you explain what the word means?
你能解釋這個字的意思嗎？

⑥ We don't know who stole the computer.
我們不知道是誰偷了電腦。

（D）由疑問形容詞所引導之名詞子句：

| 使用時機

當我們要將一個由 whose, which, what 等疑問形容詞開頭的疑問句降格成一個名詞使用時。

【句型】**S + V（+ O）+ which/what/whose + N + S + V**

① I know whose car it is.
我知道這是誰的車。

② I won't tell you which singer I like best.
我不告訴你我最喜歡的歌手是誰。

③ I don't know what pictures they are looking at.
我不知道他們在看什麼照片。

（E）由疑問副詞所引導之名詞子句：

| 使用時機

當我們要將一個由疑問副詞（如 why, how, where, when）開頭的疑問句降格成一個名詞時。

【句型】S + V + why/where/when/how + S + V

① I don't know why he hates his job.
我不知道他為何會討厭他的工作。

② They didn't tell me where they stayed last night.
他們沒有告訴我他們昨晚投宿何處。

| 名詞子句的功能

（A）當主詞：

① That Mr. Edison is a great inventor is known to everybody.
愛迪生先生是個偉大發明家，這是眾所皆知的。

② Whether your parents will agree is another question.
你父母會不會同意是另一回事。

（B）當受詞：

① Robert dreamed that he was flying to the Moon.
Robert 夢見他正飛向月球。

② I don't know if he would come back to Taiwan.
不曉得他會不會回台灣。

③ I know where he works.
我知道他在哪裡工作。

（C）當補語：

① The fact is that she doesn't like you.
事實是她並不喜歡你。

② The question is whether they will get married.
問題是他們會不會結婚。

③ What surprised me was that he cooked so well.
令我吃驚的是他的廚藝竟然如此的好。

（D）當同位語：

① We all believe the truth that he's a good man.

我們都相信他是個好人。

② The principle that men and women should be equal is known to everyone.

男女應該平等的原則是眾所皆知的。

（3）形容詞子句／關係子句：

由關係詞（包括關係代名詞如 who）所引導之附屬子句，稱為關係子句或形容詞子句，其功能在於修飾其前的名詞（稱為先行詞）。

who：先行詞是「人」時。

which：先行詞是「事」或「物」時。（which 亦可作受格用。）

where：先行詞是「地方」時。（＝in which）

whom：先行詞作受格時用。（指人）

when：先行詞是「時間」時。

why：先行詞是 the reason 時。

in which：先行詞是 the way 時。

whose：作所有格用。

that：不論先行詞為何，其關係詞皆可用 that，亦即 that 可取代 who, which, when...，但其前不可有「逗點」，亦即 that 不可用於非限定關係子句。

（A）WHO：

① I thanked the lady who helped me.

= I thanked the lady. She helped me.

我向那位幫助我的女士道謝。

② The man **who** lives next door is very mean.

= The man lives next door. He is very mean.

住在隔壁的那個男的很惡劣。

③ The guy **who**/whom/that I saw at John's party was nice.

= The guy I saw at John's party was nice.（較常用）

我在 John 的派對上看到的那個男的滿不錯的。

④ She is the woman about **whom** I told you last time.

= She is the woman **who**/whom/that I told you about last time.

= She is the woman I told you about last time.（較常用）

她就是上次我跟你說的那個女的。

（B）WHICH：

① The book **which** is on the desk is mine.

= The book on the desk is mine.（較常用）

桌上那本書是我的。

② The dog **which** is playing in the backyard is Mary's.

= The dog playing in the backyard is Mary's.（較常用）

在後院玩耍的那隻狗是 Mary 的。

③ The movie **which**/that I saw yesterday was terrible.

= The movie I saw yesterday was terrible.（較常用）

我昨天看的那部電影很爛。

④ The music to **which** I listened last night was very good.

= The music I listened to last night was very good.（較常用）

我昨晚聽的音樂很棒。

（C）WHERE：

① The building **where** Judy lives is very old.

= The building **in which** Judy lives is very old.

= The building which/that Judy lives in is very old.

= The building Judy lives in is very old.

Judy 住的那棟大樓很老舊。

② The city **where** we spent our honeymoon was beautiful.

我們度蜜月的那個城市很美。

③ That is the drawer **where** I keep my jewelry.

那個就是我放珠寶的抽屜。

（D）WHEN：

① I will never forget the day **when** I met my boyfriend.

= I'll never forget the day **on which** I met my boyfriend.

= I'll never forget the day **that** I met my boyfriend.

= I'll never forget the day I met my boyfriend.

我永難忘懷遇見我男朋友的那一天。

② 1989 was the year **when** he was killed.

一九八九年是他遇害的那一年。

（E）WHOSE：

① Yesterday I met Jim, **whose** father was my English teacher.

昨天我碰到 Jim，他爸爸是我的英文老師。

※ 注意：whose 前有逗點。

② A widow is a woman **whose** husband is dead.

寡婦就是死了丈夫的女人。

③ The girl **whose** passport was stolen is my sister-in-law.

遺失護照的那個女的是我的嫂子。

125

（F）THAT：

▌ 使用時機

（a）不想用 who, which, when 時，則用 that 取代之。

（b）其前出現最高級 (the + adj-est, the most + adj), the only, the very, the first, the last, every, all, any, no, much, little, few, everything, anything, nobody, none 等，因為太多了，不好記，所以一律用 that，就保險多了（禁忌情況除外）。

（c）其前為人和動物／事物時。

（d）其前為疑問詞，如 who。

（e）其前為強調句型：It is... that + S + V。

▌ 禁　忌

（a）that 的前面不可有介系詞。

（b）that 的前面不可出現「逗點」，亦即不可用於非限定用法。也就是其前的名詞已很明確時（如 Taiwan 只有一個，夠明確了吧？！）則不可用 that。（見 whose 的第一個例句）

① Toys **that** are dangerous should not be given to young children.

具危險性的玩具不應該給幼童玩。

※ that = which

② He is the fastest runner **that** I have ever seen.

他是我見過跑的最快的人。

※ that 在此可以省略。

③ The truck ran over a boy and his dog **that** were crossing the street.

這卡車壓死正在過馬路的一個男孩和他的狗。

④ Who **that** has a sense of honor will do it?

有榮譽感的人誰會做那種事？

⑤ It is you that I hate most.
我最恨的人就是你。

⑥ Who is the fashionable woman that came to see you yesterday?
昨天來找你的那位時髦女性是誰？

省略法
That 當受詞或主詞補語時，則可省略。

① The girl I was waiting for stood me up.
我等候的那個女孩放我鴿子。
※ **girl** 後面的 **that** 被省略。

② He is not the good boy he was.
他已不是以前那個乖小孩了。
※ **good boy** 後面的 **that** 被省略。

③ It is the only one we have in the shop.
這是我們店裡唯一的存貨了。
※ **one** 後面的 **that** 被省略。

（G）WHAT：（= the thing(s) that; the one(s) that）

① This is **what** I want.
這就是我要的東西。

② We like **what** is good.
我們喜歡好東西。

③ Tommy is not **what** he used to be.
= Tommy is not the man (that) he used to be.
= Tommy is not **what** he was.
Tommy 已不是從前的他了。

（H）-ing 子句：

① Do you know the woman talking to Jimmy?

= Do you know the woman (who is) talking to Jimmy?

你認識那個正在跟Jimmy講話的女人嗎？

② Who is the lady standing by the window?

= Who is the lady (that is) standing by the window?

那位站在窗戶邊的女士是誰？

（I）-ed 子句：

① The boy hurt in the car accident is Tim's child.

= The boy (who was) hurt in the car accident is Tim's child.

那個車禍受傷的男孩是 Tim 的孩子。

② None of the people invited to the party can come.

= None of the people (who were) invited to the party can come.

受邀的人沒有一個可以前來參加派對。

（J）WHERE, WHEN, WHY, HOW：

① This is (the place) where Mary was born.

= This is the place Mary was born.

這就是 Mary 的出生地。

② Now is (the time) when I need you most.

= Now is the time I need you most.

現在是我最需要你的時候。

③ That is (the reason) why I like you.

= That is the reason I like you.

那正是我喜歡你的原因。

④ Tell me (the way) how she did it.

= Tell me the way she did it.

告訴我她是怎麼做到的。

（K），＋關係代名詞：

此屬非限定用法，凡談論的人、事、物十分明確（如 Tom's mother, Taipei 等），則其關係代名詞前面須有逗點。而沒有逗點者，稱為限定用法。截至目前為止，幾乎你所看到的所有句子，皆屬限定用法。

① Tim's mother, who is 80, lifts weights every morning.
Tim 的母親今年八十歲了，還每天早上舉重。

② Last week I met Jenny, who told me she was getting married.
上星期我碰到 Jenny，她告訴我她快結婚了。

③ The house next to the bank, which has been empty for 10 years, has just been sold.
銀行旁邊的那間房子已空了十年，剛賣出去。

④ Last Saturday we went to Candy's party, which we enjoyed very much.
上週六我們去參加 Candy 的派對，玩得很開心。

⑤ Derek, whose mother is Taiwanese, speaks both Taiwanese and Chinese.
Derek 會講國語及台語，而他的母親是台灣人。

⑥ I don't like Linda, whose parents are so stingy.
我不喜歡 Linda，她父母很小氣。

⑦ Johnny is going to England, where his brother is working.
Johnny 要去英國，他哥哥在那裡工作。

⑧ I hate to live in Taipei, where the traffic is so heavy.
我討厭住在台北，那裡的交通很擁擠。

⑨ Fortunately they had a map, without which they would have got lost.
還好他們有地圖，要不然早就迷路了。

（L）WHICH：（修飾前面的句子）

 ① Judy couldn't come to the party, which was a pity.

  Judy 無法來參加派對，真是可惜。

 ② The weather was very bad, which we hadn't expected.

  當時天氣很糟，那是我們沒有料到的。

 ③ She said she had no time, which was not true.

  她說她沒空，根本騙人。

（M）none, all, most, neither, many, some, both, two/three... of +
which/whom

 ① Jim has 3 cars, one of which he never uses.

  = Jim has 3 cars. One of them he never uses.

  Jim 有三部車，其中一部從來沒開過。

 ② She tried on 10 dresses, none of which fitted her.

  她試穿了十件洋裝，沒有一件合身。

 ③ Kathy has a lot of friends, some of whom are rich.

  Kathy 有很多朋友，其中一些很有錢。

 ④ Jenny has two brothers, neither of whom is married.

  Jenny 有兩個兄弟，都沒有結婚。

 ⑤ June has two sisters, both of whom are not married.

  June 有兩個姊妹，只有一個結婚。

Notes

全民英語能力分級檢定測驗
初級閱讀能力測驗模擬試題

試題卷

全民英檢初級測驗一般分為 ① 聽力測驗 30 題、 ② 閱讀能力測驗 35 題及 ③ 寫作能力測驗（15 題單句寫作＋段落寫作一篇）。通過後參加複試，考口說能力測驗。以下僅就閱讀能力測驗提供部分考題，以供練習。

第一部分：詞彙和結構

1. Breakfast is _____ meal of the day.
   A. biggest
   B. the bigger
   C. more important
   D. the most important

2. It _____ me forty minutes to get to the airport yesterday.
   A. takes
   B. took
   C. spends
   D. spent

3. Mark has lived in Taipei _____ he was seven.
   A. for
   B. when
   C. since
   D. if

4. He ran away _____ the policeman came.
   A. if
   B. as soon as
   C. as long as
   D. while

5. Ken _____ in a car accident yesterday.
   A. was hurt
   B. hurt
   C. hurts
   D. was hurted

6. The shirt looks great _____ you.
   A. in
   B. on
   C. at
   D. for

7. Mark is _____ student in my class.
   A. taller
   B. tallest
   C. the taller
   D. the tallest

8. _____ you ever been to a basketball game before?
   A. Have
   B. Do
   C. Can
   D. Are

9. Please speak _____. I can't hear you.
   A. quickly
   B. sadly
   C. loudly
   D. angrily

10. It's not true _____ Judy has gone to the United States.
    A. which
    B. that
    C. this
    D. what

11. Smoking can only help us _____ for a very short time.
    A. impress
    B. comfortable
    C. interest
    D. relax

12. I should go on a _____. I've gained five kilos in a month.
    A. exercise
    B. weight
    C. subject
    D. diet

13. Please _____ at six tomorrow morning. I have to get to school early.
    A. wake me up
    B. wake up me
    C. take me up
    D. take up me

14. Jimmy is not popular at school because he likes _____.
   A. making up his mind
   B. putting on weight
   C. showing off
   D. telling jokes

15. I enjoy _____ the Internet in my free time.
   A. to surf
   B. surfing
   C. surf
   D. surfed

Question 1 - 5

Miss Lee is our English teacher. She is kind and fun to be __(1)__. Her lessons are so interesting __(2)__ the students never get bored or sleepy. She always tries __(3)__ things easy for us to understand. In class, she also likes to ask questions and gives each student a chance to answer. __(4)__ she is happy about an answer, she will nod and smile. If the answer is not correct, she will ask us to think again __(5)__ we get it right. In fact, she never embarrasses anyone in front of the class. She is really a wonderful teacher.

1. A. for
   B. with
   C. at
   D. on

2. A. when
   B. if
   C. that
   D. what

3. A. make
   B. makes
   C. making
   D. to make

4. A. While
   B. If
   C. Though
   D. As

5. A. until
   B. when
   C. as
   D. after

Question 6 - 10

> Different people have different cultures. In the United States, people are more direct in getting __(6)__ they want or asking for something. But in the east, __(7)__ China, India and Japan, people are more indirect in expressing what they think or how they want things __(8)__ .
>
> For Americans, it's common to ask, "Do you like this?" "Will you do that?" It's also OK for them to say, "I don't like it." "I won't tell you." For them, "Yes" means yes and "No" means no. But there are still some things __(9)__ Americans don't talk about with people who they don't know well. For instance, they don't ask questions like "How old are you?" "Are you married?" "How much money do you make?" "How much did your house cost?" "Who are you going to vote __(10)__?" "Why don't you have children?" and so on.

6. A. what
   B. who
   C. how
   D. where

7. A. right away
   B. more than
   C. so far
   D. such as

8. A. be done
   B. being done
   C. to be done
   D. done for

9. A. that
   B. where
   C. who
   D. what

10. A. in
    B. for
    C. at
    D. from

Question 1

> **Please wait behind the line**

1. What does this sign mean?
   A. The line is busy.
   B. Someone will see you later.
   C. Drive carefully inside the line.
   D. Do not cross the line.

Question 2

> **Do Not Run In The Hall**

2. Where will you mostly probably see this sign?
   A. In a park.
   B. On a bus.
   C. In a school.
   D. On a plane.

Question 3 - 4

Dance at Derek's High School
Open at 7:30 p.m. Dance until midnight
$150 ; $100 for Derek's students

---

3. When does the dance start?
   A. At seven o'clock.
   B. At seven thirty.
   C. At midnight.
   D. Not sure.

4. How much is it for four students of Derek's High School
   and two students of Long Life High School?
   A. $400.
   B. $500.
   C. $600.
   D. $700.

Question 5 - 6

SMART MEN'S WEAR

Item	Regular Price	Today's Price
Jeans	$1500	$999
T-shirts	$1000	$599
Socks	$200	$99
Shorts	$500	$299
Caps	$300	$199

5. How many items are on sale at Smart Men's Wear today?
   A. Four.
   B. Five.
   C. Six.
   D. Seven.

6. Judy only has two hundred and fifty dollars. What can she buy?
   A. A T-shirt.
   B. A pair of jeans.
   C. A cap or a pair of shorts.
   D. A cap or a pair of socks.

Question 7 - 8

Nina's Burgers

Hamburger	$30	Soda	$20
Cheeseburger	$40	Coffee	$30
Fishburger	$50	Tea	$30
Chickenburger	$50	Water	$20
French fries	$30	Milkshake	$40

7. What's NOT available at Nina's Burgers?
   A. Fishburgers.
   B. Milkshake.
   C. French fries.
   D. Ice Cream.

8. How much would you have to pay for two chickenburgers, two French fries, and two coffees?
   A. $200.
   B. $210.
   C. $220.
   D. $230.

Mike is reading the movie ads right now.

Movie World	
451-6616	
Superman's Back	10:00, 12:00 16:00, 19:00 21:00, 23:00

Dream Palace	
293-6633	
My Dream Woman	12:30, 15:00 17:00, 19:00 21:00, 23:00

Movie Kingdom	
451-4869	
The Bad Dream	10:00, 12:00 15:00, 17:00 19:30, 21:00

Fun Park	
903-9911	
Funny Twins	12:00, 14:30 16:30, 19:00 21:30, 23:30

9. If Mike wants to see a movie in the morning, what movie can he choose?
   A. Superman's Back or My Dream Woman.
   B. My Dream Woman or The Bad Dream.
   C. The Bad Dream or Funny Twins.
   D. Superman's Back or The Bad Dream.

10. If Mike wants to see a love story, what movie theater should he try?
    A. Movie World.
    B. Dream Palace.
    C. Movie Kingdom.
    D. Fun Park.

11. There are two movie theaters in the same area, what are they?

A. Movie World and Dream Palace.

B. Dream Palace and Movie Kingdom.

C. Movie Kingdom and Fun Park.

D. Movie World and Movie Kingdom.

Question 12 - 14

Hi Derek,

It's been two years since you left for Canada. How's everything?

You'll never guess who I saw on my way home yesterday. It was Tom Cruise, who came to Taiwan for his latest movie "Mission Impossible, Part 3." I was so excited that I couldn't get to sleep. I've been one of his fans for years. Seeing him was just like a dream come true. I asked him to sign my book. He was really handsome and friendly.

How are things in Canada? Take care!

Love,

Nina

12. **Where is Derek at the moment?**
    A. In Japan.
    B. In Canada.
    C. In Taiwan.
    D. In the United States.

13. **Where did Nina see Tom Cruise?**
    A. In the park.
    B. At the movie theater.
    C. On her way home.
    D. On the plane.

14. **What's Tom Cruise's latest movie?**
    A. Spiderman, Part 2.
    B. Cocktail.
    C. Mission Impossible, Part 3.
    D. The Day After Tomorrow.

Question 15 - 16

Do you always feel cold? Maybe you should stay in a room painted in warm colors such as red, yellow, or soft orange. Do you feel easily sad? Maybe you should sit in a yellow room. Do you often feel nervous? Maybe you should be in a blue room. Some studies show that color has the power to change our feelings. Surprisingly, colors may affect almost everyone in the same way. For instance, dark colors make people feel heavy, and bright colors make people feel light. What do you think? Do you believe these?

15. What colors can make people feel warm?
    A. blue and red.
    B. red and black.
    C. black and soft orange.
    D. soft orange and yellow.

16. What's the main idea of the reading?
    A. Colors are interesting.
    B. Colors affect people's feelings.
    C. A man will feel calm if he sits in a blue room.
    D. If you are sad, sit in a yellow room.

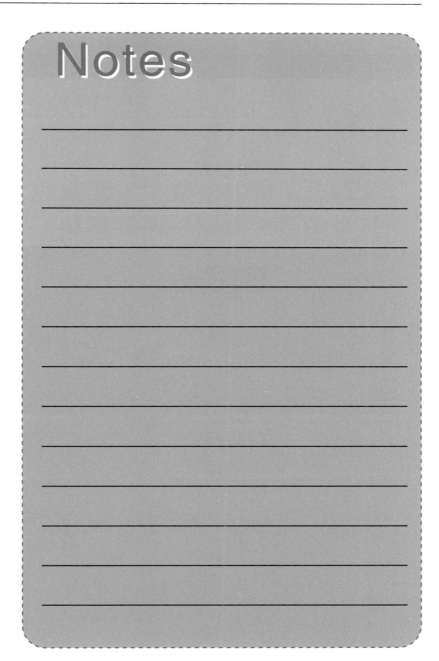

Notes

全民英語能力分級檢定測驗
初級閱讀能力測驗模擬試題

解答卷

第一部分：詞彙和結構

1. Breakfast is _____ meal of the day.
A. biggest
B. the bigger
C. more important
D. the most important

答案：（D）

中譯：早餐是一天當中最重要的一餐。

解析：由句尾 of the day 可知空格須填形容詞最高級，所以只能選 D. the most important。而選項A. 只要前面加上 the 即可。

2. It _____ me forty minutes to get to the airport yesterday.
A. takes
B. took
C. spends
D. spent

答案：（B）

中譯：我花了四十分鐘才到達機場。

解析：此題考 take 與 spend 的用法：
It takes/took（某人）＋時間＋to＋V原形
某人花…時間去…
某人spend/spent＋時間／金錢＋V-ing/on＋事物
某人花…時間／金錢去…

依此句型只能選 A. takes及 B. took。而因句尾有過去
時間 yesterday，所以只能選過去式B. took。

例句：① It took me 20 minutes to get there.
　　　　我花了二十分鐘才到那裡。
　　　② I spent two hours watching TV.
　　　　我花兩個小時看電視。
　　　③ She spent a lot of money on clothes.
　　　　她花很多錢在衣服上面。

3. Mark has lived in Taipei _____ he was seven.
　　A. for
　　B. when
　　C. since
　　D. if
答案：（C）
中譯：Mark 從七歲開始就一直住在台北。
解析：此題考 since 的用法，其句型如下：

S＋have/has＋p.p.＋since＋$\begin{cases} \text{S＋V過去式} \\ \text{過去時間} \end{cases}$

所以答案只能選 C. since。而 A. for（長達）指一段
時間，語法、語意皆不合， B. when（當），不合語
法， D. if（假如），語法、語意皆不合。

例句：① I have known her for a long time.
　　　　我認識她很久了。
　　　② He cried hard when he heard the news.
　　　　他聽到消息時，痛哭流涕。
　　　③ If you study hard, you will pass the test.
　　　　如果你用功，你就會通過考試。

4. He ran away _____ the policeman came.

   A. if

   B. as soon as

   C. as long as

   D. while

   答案：（B）

   中譯：**警察一來，他拔腿就跑。**

   解析：此題考連接詞片語 as soon as（一⋯就⋯），強調兩
   　　　個動作幾乎同時發生，所以答案只能選 B. as soon as。
   　　　而 A. if 不合語法， C. as long as（只要）不合語法，
   　　　D. while（當）不合語法。

   例句：① While I **was taking** a walk in the park, I lost my
   　　　　wallet.
   　　　　我在公園散步時，掉了皮夾。

   　　　② As long as we're together, we'll be all right.
   　　　　只要我們在一起，就不會有事的。

5. Ken _____ in a car accident yesterday.

   A. was hurt

   B. hurt

   C. hurts

   D. was hurted

   答案：（A）

   中譯：Ken 昨天車禍受傷。

   解析：此題考 hurt 的用法：

   　　　① He was hurt.
   　　　　他受傷了。

   　　　② Don't hurt him.
   　　　　別傷害他。

   　　　③ I hurt my knee (while) **playing** basketball.
   　　　　我打籃球時，傷了膝蓋。

④ My tooth hurts.
我牙痛。

⑤ It hurts my knees to run.
我跑步膝蓋會痛。

所以答案只能選 A. was hurt。

6. The shirt looks great _____ you.

A. in

B. on

C. at

D. for

答案：（B）

中譯：那件襯衫穿在你身上很好看。

解析：此題考介系詞的用法：
The shirt looks great on you.
= You look great in the shirt.

7. Mark is _____ student in my class.

A. taller

B. tallest

C. the taller

D. the tallest

答案：（D）

中譯：Mark 是我們班上最高的學生。

解析：由句尾 in my class 得知空格應填形容詞最高級，所
以只能選 D. the tallest。

8. _____ you ever been to a basketball game before?

A. Have

B. Do

C. Can

D. Are

答案：（A）

中譯：你曾經去看過籃球賽嗎？

解析：此題考現在完成式的用法：

S＋have/has＋p.p. → 疑問句：Have/Has＋S＋p.p.?

所以答案只能選 A. Have。另外由句中... been to...

亦可猜出句首空格應填 Have，因為 been 是 p.p.。

9. Please speak _____. I can't hear you.

    A. quickly

    B. sadly

    C. loudly

    D. angrily

答案：（C）

中譯：請大聲說話，我聽不見。

解析：此題考用字：

    A. quickly　快速地

    B. sadly　悲傷地

    C. loudly　大聲地

    D. angrily　生氣地

    由末句 I can't hear you.得知：只有 C. loudly 符合題意。

10. It's not true _____ Judy has gone to the United States.

    A. which

    B. that

    C. this

    D. what

答案：（B）

中譯：Judy 已經去了美國，這不是真的。

解析：此題考名詞子句的用法，句型為：

    It is＋adj＋that＋S＋V

    所以答案只能選 B. that。

11. Smoking can only help us _____ for a very short time.

A. impress

B. comfortable

C. interest

D. relax

答案：（D）

中譯：抽菸只能幫助我們放鬆一會兒。

解析：此題考 help 的用法及字義：

S + help + O +（to）V

A. impress　使印象深刻

B. comfortable　舒適的

C. interest　興趣，使⋯感到興趣

D. relax　放鬆

根據題意，此題只能選 D. relax。而 B. comfortable 不合語法。

12. I should go on a _____. I've gained five kilos in a month.

A. exercise

B. weight

C. subject

D. diet

答案：（D）

中譯：我應該要減肥／節食，我一個月內已經胖了五公斤。

解析：此題考片語 go on a diet（節食，減肥）的用法。而 A. exercise（運動）前面應接 an，而非 a，而 B. weight（重量）、C. subject（科目）皆不合題意。

13. Please _____ at six tomorrow morning. I have to get to school early.
    A. wake me up
    B. wake up me
    C. take me up
    D. take up me
    答案：（A）
    中譯：明早六點叫醒我，我必須很早到校。
    解析：此題考雙字動詞片語的用法：
        V + 介副詞（質詞）+ N = V + N + 介副詞（質詞）
        V + 代名詞 + 介副詞（質詞）
        ① Please turn on the TV.
            ＝Please turn the TV on.
            請打開電視。
        ② Please turn it on.
            請打開（它）。
        所以答案只有選項 A. wake me up 及 C. take me up
        符合語法，但依題意來看，則只有答案 A. wake me up
        可選。

14. Jimmy is not popular at school because he likes _____.
    A. making up his mind
    B. putting on weight
    C. showing off
    D. telling jokes
    答案：（C）
    中譯：Jimmy 在學校不受歡迎，因為他喜歡炫耀。
    解析：此題考片語：
        A. making up his mind   下決心，決定
        B. putting on weight   增胖，體重增加
        C. showing off   炫耀
        D. telling jokes   講笑話
        根據題意，答案只能選 C. showing off。

15. I enjoy _____ the Internet in my free time.

A. to surf

B. surfing

C. surf

D. surfed

答案：（B）

中譯：我有空時喜歡上網。

解析：此題考 enjoy 的用法：enjoy ＋ V-ing/N

　　① I enjoy listening to music.

　　　我喜歡聽音樂。

　　② I enjoyed the movie very much.

　　　我很喜歡這部電影。

Question 1 - 5

Miss Lee is our English teacher. She is kind and fun to be __(1)__ . Her lessons are so interesting __(2)__ the students never get bored or sleepy. She always tries __(3)__ things easy for us to understand. In class, she also likes to ask questions and gives each student a chance to answer. __(4)__ she is happy about an answer, she will nod and smile. If the answer is not correct, she will ask us to think again __(5)__ we get it right. In fact, she never embarrasses anyone in front of the class. She is really a wonderful teacher.

1. A. for
   B. with
   C. at
   D. on

2. A. when
   B. if
   C. that
   D. what

3. A. make
   B. makes
   C. making
   D. to make

4. A. While
   B. If
   C. Though
   D. As

5. A. until
   B. when
   C. as
   D. after

答案：
1.（B） 2.（C） 3.（D） 4.（B） 5.（A）

中譯：

> 　　李小姐是我們的英文老師。她人很好，而且跟她在一起很好玩。她的課非常有趣，所以學生從不感到無聊或想睡覺。她總是想辦法深入淺出地講課以便讓我們能了解上課的內容。在課堂上，她也喜歡問問題，同時也給每個學生機會去回答問題。如果答案令她滿意，她會點頭微笑；如果答案不對，她會要求我們再想一想，一直到我們答對為止。事實上，她從未在班上糗過任何學生。她確實是一位很棒的老師。

解析：
1. 此題考介系詞的用法：
    A. for 指「為了」或長達「一段時間」。
    　　① I did it for you.
    　　　　我為了你做這件事。
    　　② I have lived here for ten years.
    　　　　我住在這裡已經十年了。
    B. with 指「與」或「在一起」。
    　　① I went shopping with Jane.
    　　　　我和Jane去逛街。
    　　② He's fun to be with.
    　　　　跟他在一起很有趣。
    C. at 指在「小地方」或「場合」，in 則指在「大地方」或「在一個空間裡」，有時兩者互通。
    　　① He arrived at the airport at 2:30.
    　　　　他兩點半到機場。

② We had a good time at the party.
　我們在派對上玩得很開心。
③ She arrived in Japan yesterday.
　她昨天到達日本。
④ She's in her bedroom.
　她在臥室。
⑤ They're in school.
　＝They're at school.
　他們在學校。
D. on 指「在⋯之上」。
　It's on the table.
　東西在桌上。

2. 此題考 so... that...（如此⋯以致於⋯）的用法：
① He is so young that he can't go to school.
　他年紀是如此的小以致於不能上學。
　＝He is too young to go to school.
　他年紀太小而不能上學。
② He walked so quickly that we couldn't catch up with him.
　他走得如此地快以致於我們趕不上他。
　＝He walked too quickly for us to catch up with.
　他走太快了，我們趕不上。（※ 句尾不可加 him）

3. 此題考 try 的用法：
　try to＋V　試圖，努力去⋯
　try＋V-ing　試試看
① He tried to help his friend.
　他努力去幫助朋友。
② It's so hot. Try turning on the fan.
　天氣好熱，打開電扇看會不會好一點。
由上下文得知，答案應選 D. to make。

159

4. 此題考連接詞的用法：

　A. While 指「當」。

　　While I was running in the park, I met my English teacher.

　　我在公園跑步時，遇見了我的英文老師。

　B. If 指「如果」。

　　If you are good at English, you will have more job opportunities.

　　你如果英文好，你就有更多的工作機會。

　C. Though 指「雖然」，等於 Although。

　　Though he's poor, he's very happy.

　　他雖然窮，但很快樂。

　D. As 指「當」或「因為」。

　　① As I went to school today, I saw an accident.

　　　當我今天去上學時，我看見一場意外。

　　② As I was sick, I didn't go to school.

　　　因為生病，所以我沒去學校。

　根據上下文，答案應選 B. If。

5. 此題考連接詞的用法：

　A. until　直到，可當連接詞或介系詞，等於口語的 till。

　　① I'll wait until he **comes**.

　　　我要等到他來。

　　　※ until 後面的子句，須用現在式代替未來式，如此句的

　　　　comes，<u>不可用</u> **will come**。

　　② I didn't go to bed until 2:30 a.m.

　　　我直到凌晨兩點半才去睡覺。

　B. when　當

　C. as　當；因為

　D. after　在…之後

　根據題意，答案應選 A. until（直到）。

Different people have different cultures. In the United States, people are more direct in getting __(6)__ they want or asking for something. But in the east, __(7)__ China, India and Japan, people are more indirect in expressing what they think or how they want things __(8)__ .

For Americans, it's common to ask, "Do you like this?" "Will you do that?" It's also OK for them to say, "I don't like it." "I won't tell you." For them, "Yes" means yes and "No" means no. But there are still some things __(9)__ Americans don't talk about with people who they don't know well. For instance, they don't ask questions like "How old are you?" "Are you married?" "How much money do you make?" "How much did your house cost?" "Who are you going to vote __(10)__ ?" "Why don't you have children?" and so on.

6. A. what
   B. who
   C. how
   D. where

7. A. right away
   B. more than
   C. so far
   D. such as

8. A. be done
   B. being done
   C. to be done
   D. done for

9. A. that
   B. where
   C. who
   D. what

10. A. in
    B. for
    C. at
    D. from

答案：

6.（A） 7.（D） 8.（C） 9.（A） 10.（B）

中譯：

> 　　不同的人有不同的文化。在美國，人們對自己的需求表達比較直接。可是在東方，像是中國、日本和印度，人們在表達自己的思想及需求上就比較間接。
>
> 　　對美國人來說，問對方「你喜歡嗎？」「你願意做嗎？」是很稀鬆平常的事。同樣地，回應對方「我不喜歡。」「我不告訴你。」也無妨。對老美來說，是就是，不是就不是。但是對不熟的人，他們還是有些避諱。比如說，他們不會問這類的問題：「你幾歲？」「你結婚了沒？」「你的薪水是多少？」「你的房子是多少錢買的？」「你要投票給誰？」「你怎麼沒有小孩？」等等。

解析：

5. 此題考指示代名詞 what的用法：

　　① This is what I want.

　　　　＝This is the thing that I want.

　　　　這就是我要的。（此為關係代名詞的變形）

　　② Tell me what you need.（屬間接敘述）

　　　　＝What do you need? Tell me.（屬直接敘述）

　　　　告訴我你需要什麼。

　　③ I don't know who they want.（屬間接敘述）

　　　　＝Who do they want? I don't know.（屬直接敘述）

　　　　我不知道他們要誰。

　　④ Tell me how they want it.（屬間接敘述）

　　　　＝How do they want it? Tell me.（屬直接敘述）

　　　　告訴我他們要如何做。

⑤ I don't know where she lives.（屬間接敘述）

　＝Where does she live? I don't know.（屬直接敘述）

　我不知道她住在哪裡。

綜合上述，可知只有 A. what 符合語法及題意。

7. 此題考片語用法：

　A. right away：立刻，等於at once, immediately。

　B. more than：超過，等於over。

　C. so far：迄今，一般用於現在完成式。

　　I **have read** ten books so far.

　　到目前為止，我已經讀了十本書。

　D. such as (= like)：像是，例如。

　綜合上述，可知答案為 D. such as。

8. 此題考文法「間接敘述」動詞 **want** 及被動式的用法：

　Tell me how they want it to be done.（屬間接敘述）

　＝How do they want it to be done? Tell me.（屬直接敘述）

　告訴我他們要如何做這件事。

　根據上述，答案只能選 C. to be done。

9. 此題考關係代名詞的用法：（詳情請參考文法重點整理）

　who：先行詞為人。

　which：先行詞為事、物。

　where：先行詞為地方。

　that：先行詞為人、事、物…，但前面不可有逗號。

　由於先行詞為 some things，所以關係代名詞只能用 which

　或 A. that。

10. 此題考 **vote** 的用法：

　vote for：投票給…，投票贊成。

　vote against：不投票給…，投票反對。

　依題意答案只能選 B. for。

第三部分：閱讀理解

Question 1

> • **Please wait behind the line** •

1. What does this sign mean?
   A. The line is busy.
   B. Someone will see you later.
   C. Drive carefully inside the line.
   D. Do not cross the line.

第 1 題

> • 請 在 線 後 等 待 •

1. 題目：這個標誌是什麼意思？
   選項：A. 線路很忙。
   　　　B. 待會兒有人會來看你。
   　　　C. 請在線內小心駕駛。
   　　　D. 請勿越線。
   答案：(D)

Question 2

```
●    Do Not Run In The Hall    ●
```

2. Where will you mostly probably see this sign?
   A. In a park.
   B. On a bus.
   C. In a school.
   D. On a plane.

第 2 題

```
●    請 勿 在 走 廊 上 跑 步    ●
```

2. 題目：這個標誌最可能出現的地點為何？
   選項：A. 公園。
         B. 公車上。
         C. 學校。
         D. 飛機上。
   答案：（C）

Question 3 - 4

> *Dance at Derek's High School*
> *Open at 7:30 p.m. Dance until midnight*
> *$150 ; $100 for Derek's students*

3. When does the dance start?
   A. At seven o'clock.
   B. At seven thirty.
   C. At midnight.
   D. Not sure.

4. How much is it for four students of Derek's High School and two students of Long Life High School?
   A. $400.
   B. $500.
   C. $600.
   D. $700.

Derek 高 中 舞 會
晚上七點半開始　瘋狂到午夜
入場卷：150元　本校學生：100元

---

3. 題目：**舞會何時開始？**
　　選項：A. 七點。
　　　　　B. 七點半。
　　　　　C. 午夜。
　　　　　D. 不確定。
　　答案：（B）

4. 題目：**如果四個 Derek 高中的學生和兩個 Long Life 高中的學生來跳舞，那麼他們要付多少錢？**
　　選項：A. 四百元。
　　　　　B. 五百元。
　　　　　C. 六百元。
　　　　　D. 七百元。
　　答案：（D）

Question 5 - 6

SMART MEN'S WEAR		
Item	Regular Price	*Today's Price*
Jeans	$1500	*$999*
T-shirts	$1000	*$599*
Socks	$200	*$99*
Shorts	$500	*$299*
Caps	$300	*$199*

5. How many items are on sale at Smart Men's Wear today?

A. Four.

B. Five.

C. Six.

D. Seven.

6. Judy only has two hundred and fifty dollars. What can she buy?

A. A T-shirt.

B. A pair of jeans.

C. A cap or a pair of shorts.

D. A cap or a pair of socks.

第 5 - 6 題

```
聰 明 男 子 服 飾 店
項目          平常價格          今天的價格
牛仔褲         1500 元            999 元
T恤           1000 元            599 元
襪子           200 元             99 元
短褲           500 元            299 元
鴨舌帽          300 元            199 元
```

5. 題目：聰明男子服飾店今日的特價品有幾項？
   選項：A. 四。
         B. 五。
         C. 六。
         D. 七。
   答案：（B）

6. 題目：Judy 身上只有二百五十元，她可以買什麼東西？
   選項：A. 一件 T 恤。
         B. 一件牛仔褲。
         C. 一頂鴨舌帽或一件短褲。
         D. 一頂鴨舌帽或一雙襪子。
   答案：（D）

Question 7 - 8

Nina's Burgers

Hamburger	$30	Soda	$20
Cheeseburger	$40	Coffee	$30
Fishburger	$50	Tea	$30
Chickenburger	$50	Water	$20
French fries	$30	Milkshake	$40

7. What's NOT available at Nina's Burgers?
   A. Fishburgers.
   B. Milkshake.
   C. French fries.
   D. Ice Cream.

8. How much would you have to pay for two chickenburgers, two French fries, and two coffees?
   A. $200.
   B. $210.
   C. $220.
   D. $230.

Nina 漢堡店

漢　堡	30元	汽　水	20元
吉士堡	40元	咖　啡	30元
魚　堡	50元	紅　茶	30元
雞肉堡	50元	礦泉水	20元
薯　條	30元	奶　昔	40元

7. 題目：Nina 漢堡店沒有賣什麼東西？
　　選項：A. 魚堡。
　　　　　B. 奶昔。
　　　　　C. 薯條。
　　　　　D. 冰淇淋。
　　答案：（D）

8. 題目：**兩份雞肉堡、兩份薯條和兩杯咖啡總共要多少錢？**
　　選項：A. 200元。
　　　　　B. 210元。
　　　　　C. 220元。
　　　　　D. 230元。
　　答案：（C）

Question 9 - 11

Mike is reading the movie ads right now.

Movie World	
451-6616	
Superman's Back	10:00, 12:00 16:00, 19:00 21:00, 23:00

Dream Palace	
293-6633	
My Dream Woman	12:30, 15:00 17:00, 19:00 21:00, 23:00

Movie Kingdom	
451-4869	
The Bad Dream	10:00, 12:00 15:00, 17:00 19:30, 21:00

Fun Park	
903-9911	
Funny Twins	12:00, 14:30 16:30, 19:00 21:30, 23:30

9. If Mike wants to see a movie in the morning, what movie can he choose?
   A. Superman's Back or My Dream Woman.
   B. My Dream Woman or The Bad Dream.
   C. The Bad Dream or Funny Twins.
   D. Superman's Back or The Bad Dream.

10. If Mike wants to see a love story, what movie theater should he try?
    A. Movie World.
    B. Dream Palace.
    C. Movie Kingdom.
    D. Fun Park.

11. There are two movie theaters in the same area, what are they?
   A. Movie World and Dream Palace.
   B. Dream Palace and Movie Kingdom.
   C. Movie Kingdom and Fun Park.
   D. Movie World and Movie Kingdom.

第 9 - 11 題

Mike 正在看電影廣告。

電　影　世　界	
451-6616	
再見超人	10:00, 12:00 16:00, 19:00 21:00, 23:00

夢　幻　宮　殿	
293-6633	
我的夢中情人	12:30, 15:00 17:00, 19:00 21:00, 23:00

電　影　王　國	
451-4869	
惡　夢	10:00, 12:00 15:00, 17:00 19:30, 21:00

歡　樂　公　園	
903-9911	
搞笑雙胞胎	12:00, 14:30 16:30, 19:00 21:30, 23:30

9. 題目：如果 Mike 想看早場的電影，那麼他可以選擇哪部電影？
   選項：A. 再見超人或我的夢中情人。
   　　　B. 我的夢中情人或惡夢。
   　　　C. 惡夢或搞笑雙胞胎。
   　　　D. 再見超人或惡夢。
   答案：（D）

10. 題目：如果 Mike 想看文藝片，那麼他應該試試哪家戲院？
    選項：A. 電影世界。
    　　　B. 夢幻宮殿。
    　　　C. 電影王國。
    　　　D. 歡樂公園。
    答案：（B）

11. 題目：有兩家戲院屬於同一個地區，是哪兩家？
    選項：A. 電影世界和夢幻宮殿。
    　　　B. 夢幻宮殿和電影王國。
    　　　C. 電影王國和歡樂公園。
    　　　D. 電影世界和電影王國。
    答案：（D）
    　　　※ 由電話（451-）判別所屬區域得知。

Question 12 - 14

Hi Derek,

It's been two years since you left for Canada. How's everything?

You'll never guess who I saw on my way home yesterday. It was Tom Cruise, who came to Taiwan for his latest movie "Mission Impossible, Part 3." I was so excited that I couldn't get to sleep. I've been one of his fans for years. Seeing him was just like a dream come true. I asked him to sign my book. He was really handsome and friendly.

How are things in Canada? Take care!

Love,
Nina

---

12. Where is Derek at the moment?
   A. In Japan.
   B. In Canada.
   C. In Taiwan.
   D. In the United States.

13. Where did Nina see Tom Cruise?
   A. In the park.
   B. At the movie theater.
   C. On her way home.
   D. On the plane.

14. What's Tom Cruise's latest movie?

　　A. Spiderman, Part 2.

　　B. Cocktail.

　　C. Mission Impossible, Part 3.

　　D. The Day After Tomorrow.

第 12 - 14 題

親愛的 Derek：

　　你去加拿大到現在已有兩年了，一切可好？

　　你絕對猜不到我昨天在回家路上遇到誰了！是阿湯哥（Tom Cruise）！他來台灣宣傳他最新的電影「不可能的任務第三集」。我興奮得睡不著覺。多年以來我一直是他的影迷，看見他彷彿美夢成真。我要求他在我的書本上簽名。他真的又帥又親切呢！

　　加拿大一切可好？保重喔！

愛你的
Nina

12. 題目：此刻 Derek 人在哪裡？
    選項：A. 在日本。
          B. 在加拿大。
          C. 在台灣。
          D. 在美國。
    答案：（B）

13. 題目：Nina 在哪裡遇見阿湯哥（Tom Cruise）？
    選項：A. 在公園。
          B. 在戲院。
          C. 在回家路上。
          D. 在飛機上。
    答案：（C）

14. 題目：阿湯哥最新的電影是什麼？
    選項：A. 蜘蛛人第二集。
          B. 雞尾酒。
          C. 不可能的任務第三集。
          D. 明天過後。
    答案：（C）

Question 15 - 16

Do you always feel cold? Maybe you should stay in a room painted in warm colors such as red, yellow, or soft orange. Do you feel easily sad? Maybe you should sit in a yellow room. Do you often feel nervous? Maybe you should be in a blue room. Some studies show that color has the power to change our feelings. Surprisingly, colors may affect almost everyone in the same way. For instance, dark colors make people feel heavy, and bright colors make people feel light. What do you think? Do you believe these?

15. What colors can make people feel warm?
    A. blue and red.
    B. red and black.
    C. black and soft orange.
    D. soft orange and yellow.

16. What's the main idea of the reading?
    A. Colors are interesting.
    B. Colors affect people's feelings.
    C. A man will feel calm if he sits in a blue room.
    D. If you are sad, sit in a yellow room.

> 　　你總是感到寒冷嗎？也許你應該待在漆有暖色調如紅色、黃色或淺橘色的房間內。你很容易感到哀傷嗎？也許你應該坐在黃色的房間裡。你經常感到緊張嗎？也許你應該待在藍色的房間裡。有些研究報告指出：顏色具有改變我們情緒的力量。令人吃驚的是，顏色對每個人的影響幾乎是一樣的。例如：深色使人感到沈重，而淺色使人感覺輕鬆。你認為呢？你相信這些說法嗎？

15. 題目：什麼顏色會使人感到溫暖？
　　選項：A. 藍色和紅色。
　　　　　B. 紅色和黑色。
　　　　　C. 黑色和柔橘。
　　　　　D. 柔橘和黃色。
　　答案：（D）

16. 題目：這篇文章的主旨為何？
　　選項：A. 顏色是有趣的。
　　　　　B. 顏色會改變人的情緒。
　　　　　C. 一個人如果坐在藍色的房間裡，那他會感到平靜。
　　　　　D. 如果你難過，那就待在黃色的房間。
　　答案：（B）

寫作能力測驗

Writing Test

第一章 寫作題型全都錄

1 句子改寫

壹、直述句與疑問句、答句之改寫

1. Your father is an English teacher.
   Is _____?
   答案：Is your father an English teacher?
   中譯：你父親是英文老師嗎？

2. She wants to go shopping.
   Does _____?
   答案：Does she want to go shopping?
   中譯：她要去逛街嗎？

3. They come here every Sunday.
   Do _____?
   答案：Do they come here every Sunday?
   中譯：他們每個禮拜天都來這裡嗎？

4. He gave Mary some books.
   Did _____?
   答案：Did he give Mary some books?
   中譯：他給了 Mary 一些書嗎？

5. John will go to Japan.
   Will _____?
   答案：Will John go to Japan?
   中譯：John 要去日本嗎？

6. We should invite Susan to our party.
   Should _____?
   答案：Should we invite Susan to our party?
   中譯：我們要邀請 Susan 來參加派對嗎？

7. Lucy can do the job well.

   Can _____?

   答案：Can Lucy do the job well?

   中譯：Lucy 可以勝任這個工作嗎？

8. They are going to play basketball tomorrow.

   Are _____?

   答案：Are they going to play basketball tomorrow?

   中譯：他們明天要去打籃球嗎？

9. Mary hasn't finished her homework yet.

   Has _____?

   答案：Has Mary finished her homework yet?

   中譯：Mary 已經寫完功課了嗎？

10. She has never been to Hong Kong.

    Has _____?

    答案：Has she ever been to Hong Kong (before)?

    中譯：她以前去過香港嗎？

11. Judy gets up at 6:30 every day.

    When _____?

    答案：When does Judy get up every day?

    中譯：Judy 每天幾點起床？

12. John took the test yesterday.

    When _____?

    答案：When did John take the test?

    中譯：John 何時考試？

13. Derek and Nina will go to France next year.

When _____?

答案：When will Derek and Nina go to France?

中譯：Derek 和 Nina 何時要去法國？

14. Eva is going to America this summer.

When _____?

答案：When is Eva going to America?

中譯：Eva 何時要去美國？

15. How do you go to school?

I _____.

答案：I go to school on foot.　I go to school by bus.

中譯：我走路上學。　我搭公車上學。

16. How did you go to the zoo?

I _____.

答案：I went to the zoo by MRT.

中譯：我搭捷運去動物園。

17. How will you go to the airport?

I _____.

答案：I will go to the airport by taxi.

中譯：我將搭計程車去機場。

18. How often do you play tennis?

I _____.

答案：I play tennis twice a week.

中譯：我每週打兩次網球。

19. How many people are there in your family?

    There _____.

    答案：There are five people in my family.

    中譯：我家裡有五個人。

20. How much does it cost?

    It _____.

    答案：It costs $150.

    中譯：那個要一百五十元。

21. It took Jessie twenty minutes to get there.

    How _____?

    答案：How long did it take Jessie to get there?

    中譯：Jessie 花多久時間才到那裡？

22. Mr. Smith goes to work by car every day.

    How _____?

    答案：How does Mr. Smith go to work every day?

    中譯：Smith 先生每天如何去上班？（搭何種交通工具？）

23. Judy visits her grandmother once a month.

    How _____?

    答案：How often does Judy visit her grandmother?

    中譯：Judy 多久去探望她的奶奶？

24. He has been working here for three years.

    How _____?

    答案：How long has he been working here?

    中譯：他在這裡工作多久了？

25. Mary is watching TV now.

    What _____?

    答案：What is Mary doing now?

    中譯：Mary 現在在做什麼？

26. Mike was at the beach yesterday.

    Where _____?

    答案：Where was Mike yesterday?

    中譯：Mike 昨天人在哪裡？

27. There are 150 workers in this factory.

    How _____?

    答案：How many workers are there in this factory?

    中譯：這家工廠有多少個工人？

28. The watch cost me $5000.

    How _____?

    答案：How much did the watch cost (you)?

    中譯：這隻手錶你花了多少錢買的？

29. I spent $2000 on the T-shirt.

    How _____?

    答案：How much did you spend on the T-shirt?

    中譯：你花了多少錢買這件 T 恤？

30. I was cooking when May called yesterday.

    What _____?

    答案：What were you doing when May called yesterday?

    中譯：昨天 May 打電話來的時候，你在做什麼？

1. This is a banana.

   These _____.

   答案：These are bananas.

   中譯：這些是香蕉。

2. He is a police officer.

   They _____.

   答案：They are police officers.

   中譯：他們是警察。

3. That is an excellent book.

   Those _____.

   答案：Those are excellent books.

   中譯：那些是很棒的書。

4. It is a great song.

   They _____.

   答案：They are great songs.

   中譯：那些是很棒的歌。

1. I live in Taipei.

   Lucy _____.

   答案：Lucy lives in Taipei.

   中譯：Lucy 住在台北。

2. They have a cute dog.

   Michael _____.

   答案：Michael has a cute dog.

   中譯：Michael 有一隻可愛的狗。

3. I was at the party last night.

   They _____.

   答案：They were at the party last night.

   中譯：他們昨晚去參加派對。

肆、時態改寫

1. I usually go to school by bus.

   I _____yesterday.

   答案：I went to school by bus yesterday.

   中譯：我昨天搭公車去上學。

2. They went shopping last week.

   They _____. （用 next week）

   答案：They will go shopping next week.

   　　　= They are going to go shopping next week.

   中譯：他們下週要去逛街。

3. Will you join the basketball team?

   Are _____?

   答案：Are you going to join the basketball team?

   中譯：你打算加入籃球隊嗎？

4. Judy practices the piano every day.

Judy _____now.

答案：Judy is practicing the piano now.

中譯：Judy 現在正在彈鋼琴。

5. Bill went swimming last night.

Bill _____every day.

答案：Bill goes swimming every day.

中譯：Bill 每天去游泳。

伍、主動與被動之改寫

1. Did Coco clean the room last night?

Was _____?

答案：Was the room cleaned by Coco last night?

中譯：這房間昨天是由 Coco 打掃的嗎？

2. Lulu will do the job tomorrow.

The job _____.

答案：The job will be done by Lulu tomorrow.

中譯：這工作明天將由 Lulu 來做。

3. They are building a new bridge there.

A new bridge _____.

答案：A new bridge is being built by them there.

中譯：有一座新橋正由他們在那裡搭建。

（他們正在那裡搭建一座新橋。）

4. The policeman has caught the thief.

The thief _____.

答案：The thief has been caught by the policeman.

中譯：小偷已經被警察逮捕。

5. Pop music really interests me.

I _____.

答案：I am really interested in pop music.

中譯：我對流行音樂的確有興趣。

6. The news really surprised me.

I _____.

答案：I was really surprised at the news.

中譯：聽到這消息，我真的很吃驚。

陸、虛主詞（It）與真主詞（動名詞、不定詞）之改寫

1. Learning English songs is fun.

It _____.

答案：It is fun to learn English songs.

= It is fun learning English songs.

= To learn English songs is fun.

中譯：學英文歌很有趣。

2. To speak English well is my dream.

It _____.

答案：It is my dream to speak English well.

= It is my dream speaking English well.

= Speaking English well is my dream.

中譯：說一口好英語是我的夢想。

※ to speak English well = to speak good English

3. It is necessary to obey traffic rules.

To _____.

答案：To obey traffic rules is necessary.

= Obeying traffic rules is necessary.

中譯：我們必須遵守交通規則。

4. It was a lot of trouble finding your apartment.

Finding _____.

答案：Finding your apartment was a lot of trouble.

中譯：你的公寓很難找。

柒、直接敘述與間接敘述之改寫

1. What do you want?

I don't know _____.

答案：I don't know what you want.

中譯：我不知道你要什麼。

2. Where does John live?

Do you know _____?

答案：Do you know where John lives?

中譯：你知道John住哪裡嗎？

3. Where are you from?

Tell me _____.

答案：Tell me where you are from.

中譯：告訴我你從哪裡來。

4. Can we win the game?

I don't know _____.

答案：I don't know whether we can win the game.

= I don't know if we can win the game.

= I don't know whether we can win the game or not.

= I don't know whether or not we can win the game.

中譯：我不知道我們是否會贏得比賽。

5. She said to Tim, "Where do you work?"

She asked Tim _____.

答案：She asked Tim where he worked.

中譯：她問 Tim 他在哪裡工作？

6. Mother said to me, "Don't watch TV too late."

Mother told me _____.

答案：Mother told me not to watch TV too late.

中譯：媽媽叫我不要看電視看得太晚。

7. He said, "Do you have a pen?"

He asked me _____.

答案：He asked me if I had a pen.

= He asked me whether I had a pen.

= He asked me whether I had a pen or not.

= He asked me whether or not I had a pen.

中譯：他問我有沒有筆。

捌、比較級、最高級與原級之改寫

1. Tom is taller than Peter.

   Peter _____.

   答案：Peter is shorter than Tom.

   中譯：Peter 比 Tom 矮。

2. Tina is thin, and Linda is thin, too.（用 as... as）

   Tina _____.

   答案：Tina is as thin as Linda.

   中譯：Tina 和 Linda 一樣瘦。

3. John's car is cheaper than mine.

   My car _____.

   答案：My car is more expensive than John's.

   中譯：我的車比 John 的要貴。

4. John's apartment is not as cheap as Mary's.

   Mary's apartment _____.

   答案：Mary's apartment is cheaper than John's.

   　　　= Mary's apartment is less expensive than John's.

   中譯：Mary的公寓比John的便宜。

5. Taipei is more crowded than any other city in Taiwan.

   （用最高級形容詞）

   Taipei _____.

   答案：Taipei is the most crowded city in Taiwan.

   中譯：台北是台灣最擁擠的城市。

6. No other student is taller than Joe in his class.（用最高級形容詞）
   Joe _____.
   答案：Joe is the tallest student in his class.
   　　　= Joe is taller than any other student in his class.
   　　　（比較級）
   　　　= Joe is taller than everyone else in his class.（比較級）
   　　　= Joe is taller than all the other students in his class.
   　　　（比較級）
   中譯：Joe 是他班上最高的學生。

7. Mark talks the fastest in the family.（用比較級形容詞）
   Mark _____.
   答案：Mark talks faster than any other member in the family.
   　　　= Mark talks faster than everyone else in the family.
   　　　= Mark talks faster than all the other members in the family.
   中譯：Mark 是家中說話最快的一員。

8. Derek speaks English better than everyone else in his class.
   （用最高級形容詞）
   Derek _____.
   答案：Derek speaks English the best in his class.
   中譯：Derek 是他班上英語說得最棒的一個學生。

玖、其他句型之改寫

1. I was late for school yesterday because I missed the train.
   I _____, so _____.
   答案：I missed the train, so I was late for school yesterday.
   中譯：我沒搭上火車，所以昨天上學遲到。

2. Though Johnny is poor, he is very happy.

   Johnny _____.

   答案：Johnny is poor, but he is very happy.

   　　　或：Johnny is very happy though he is poor.

   中譯：雖然 Johnny 沒有錢，但是他很快樂。

3. Why don't we try that new cafe?

   How about _____?

   答案：How about trying that new cafe?

   中譯：我們去試試那家新咖啡廳好嗎？

4. The story is interesting to me.

   I _____.

   答案：I am interested in the story.

   中譯：我對這個故事很有興趣。

5. The show was boring to me.

   I _____.

   答案：I was bored with the show.

   中譯：我覺得這個表演很無聊。

6. Mimi spent two thousand dollars on this dress.

   This dress _____.

   答案：This dress cost Mimi two thousand dollars.

   中譯：這件洋裝花了 Mimi 兩千元。

7. Tony is too young to go to school.

   Tony isn't _____.

   答案：Tony isn't old enough to go to school.

   　　　= Tony is so young that he can't go to school.

   中譯：Tony年紀太小而不能去上學。

8. Andy is from Hong Kong, and I am, too.（用 so...）
   Andy _____.
   答案：Andy is from Hong Kong, and so am I.
   中譯：Andy 是從香港來的，我也是。

9. The bike is not the same as mine.（用 different）
   The bike _____.
   答案：The bike is different from mine.
   中譯：這台腳踏車跟我的不一樣。

10. Coco didn't call her mother yesterday.
    Coco forgot _____.
    答案：Coco forgot to call her mother yesterday.
    中譯：Coco 昨天忘記打電話給她媽媽。

11. If you work harder, you'll pass the test.
    Work _____.
    答案：Work harder, and you'll pass the test.
    中譯：用功一點，你就會通過考試。

12. If you don't study hard, you can't pass the test.（用 without）
    You can't _____.
    答案：You can't pass the test without studying hard.
    中譯：不用功你就沒有辦法通過考試。

13. Can you lend me one hundred dollars?
    May I _____?
    答案：May I borrow one hundred dollars from you?
    　　　 = Can you lend one hundred dollars to me?
    中譯：我可以跟你借一百元嗎？

14. Nina is a beautiful girl.

What _____!

答案：What a beautiful girl Nina is!

= How beautiful a girl Nina is!

= How beautiful Nina is!

中譯：Nina 真是漂亮啊！

15. Mother: Did you clean the table?

Tommy: Oh, no!

Tommy forgot _____.

答案：Tommy forgot to clean the table.

中譯：Tommy 忘了清理桌子。

16. I have something to tell you .（加入 important）

I _____.

答案：I have something important to tell you.

中譯：我有重要的事要告訴你。

17. Why don't you go swimming?

Why not _____?

答案：Why not go swimming?

中譯：何不去游泳呢？

18. You look great in the new dress.

The new dress _____.

答案：The new dress looks great on you.

中譯：這件洋裝穿在你身上真是好看！

2 句子合併

壹、對等連接詞之合併

1. Nina likes to go shopping.
   Nina likes to surf the Internet.

   _____.

   答案：Nina likes to go shopping and surf the Internet.
   中譯：Nina 喜歡去逛街和上網。

2. John wants to take the test.
   He doesn't want to write a report.

   _____.

   答案：John wants to take the test, but he doesn't want to write a
   report.
   中譯：John 想要考試，但他不想要寫報告。

3. You can pay cash.
   You can use a credit card.

   _____.

   答案：You can pay cash or use a credit card.
   中譯：你可以付現或刷卡。

4. Lisa can't type.
   She can't speak English, either.（用 neither... nor...）

   _____.

   答案：Lisa can neither type nor speak English.
   中譯：Lisa 不會打字，也不會說英語。

5. I'll pick you up at the station.

  You go by taxi.（用 either...or...）

  _____.

  答案：Either I'll pick you up at the station or you go by taxi.

  中譯：不是我去車站接你，就是你自己搭計程車去。

6. Lucy enjoys listening to music.

  Candy enjoys listening to music, too.（用 not only... but also...）

  _____.

  答案：Not only Lucy but also Candy enjoys listening to music.

  中譯：喜歡聽音樂的不只是 Lucy，還有 Candy。

7. Eva can't swim.

  Jessie can't swim.（用 nor）

  _____.

  答案：Eva can't swim, and nor can Jessie.

  　　　= Eva can't swim, and neither can Jessie.

  中譯：Eva 不會游泳，Jessie 也不會。

  ※ nor, neither 須倒裝。

貳、以時態合併

1. Cathy was in the hospital two weeks ago.

  She is still in the hospital now.（用 since）

  _____.

  答案：Cathy has been in the hospital since two weeks ago.

  中譯：Cathy 住院已經有兩週時間了。

2. I will get to Hong Kong.

　　Then I will call you.（用 as soon as）

_____.

　答案：As soon as I get to Hong Kong, I will call you.

　　　　或 I'll call you as soon as I get to Hong Kong.

　中譯：我一到香港，我就打電話給你。

3.　We were eating dinner.

　　John arrived.（用 when）

_____.

　答案：We were eating dinner when John arrived.

　　　　或 When John arrived, we were eating dinner.

　中譯：John 到的時候，我們正在吃晚飯。

<h2 style="text-align:center">參、以介系詞合併</h2>

1. Michael makes much money.

　　He sells used cars.（用 by）

_____.

　答案：Michael makes much money by selling used cars.

　中譯：Michael 靠著賣中古車賺了很多錢。

　※　used = second-hand：二手的。

2. You can't play computer games.

　　You should finish your homework.（用 without）

_____.

　答案：You can't play computer games without finishing your
　　　　homework.

　中譯：你要做完功課才能玩電腦遊戲。

肆、以名詞子句合併

1. Please tell me something.
   You're late again.（用 why）

   _____.

   答案：Please tell me why you're late again.
   中譯：請告訴我為什麼你又遲到。

2. I want to know something.
   Where does Michael live?

   _____.

   答案：I want to know where Michael lives.
   中譯：我要知道 Michael 住在哪裡。

3. Why did Coco leave for Canada?
   No one knows.

   _____.

   答案：No one knows why Coco left for Canada.
   中譯：沒有人知道 Coco 前往加拿大的原因。

4. She asked me a question.
   The question was, "Are you from China?"（用 whether）

   _____.

   答案：She asked me whether I was from China.
   　　　= She asked me if I was from China.
   中譯：她問我是不是從中國來的。

伍、以副詞子句合併

1. The man is very weak.

   He can't get out of bed by himself.（用 so... that...）

   _____.

   答案：The man is so weak that he can't get out of bed by himself.
   中譯：這個男的身體太虛弱，以至於無法自己下床。

2. Nancy studies in the best school in Taipei.

   She is not happy.（用 though）

   _____.

   答案：Though Nancy studies in the best school in Taipei, she is
   　　　not happy.
   　　　= Nancy is not happy though she studies in the best school
   　　　　in Taipei.
   中譯：雖然 Nancy 就讀於台北最好的學校，可是她並不快樂。

陸、以形容詞子句合併

1. Andy is an American businessman.

   He speaks Chinese very well.（用 who）

   _____.

   答案：Andy is an American businessman who speaks Chinese
   　　　very well.
   中譯：Andy 是一個很會講中文的美國商人。

2. I know a man.

The man's mother is a great artist.（用 whose）

_____.

答案：I know a man whose mother is a great artist.

中譯：我認識一個男的，他母親是個偉大的藝術家。

3. This is a book.

I've found many mistakes in it.（用 in which）

_____.

答案：This is a book in which I've found many mistakes.

中譯：這是一本我發現裡面有很多錯誤的書。

4. The city was beautiful.

We spent our honeymoon there.（用 where）

_____.

答案：The city where we spent our honeymoon was beautiful.

中譯：我們去渡蜜月的那座城市很美。

5. I live in an apartment.

The apartment is big but cheap.（用 which）

_____.

答案：I live in an apartment which is big but cheap.

中譯：我住在一間很大但不貴的公寓。

6. Michael didn't go to school yesterday.

It made his parents very angry.

_____.

答案：Michael didn't go to school yesterday, which made his parents very angry.

中譯：Michael 昨天沒去上學，這件事讓他爸媽很生氣。

柒、以比較級、最高級與原級合併

1. Jack is 160cm tall.
   Mike is 160cm tall.（用 as... as）

   _____.
   答案：Jack is as tall as Mike.
   中譯：Jack 和 Mike 一樣高。

2. Lisa is taller than Judy.
   Judy is taller than Jenny.（用最高級）

   _____.
   答案：Lisa is the tallest of the three (girls).
   中譯：Lisa 是三個女孩當中最高的一個。

3. This watch is cheap.
   That watch is very cheap.（用比較級）

   _____.
   答案：That watch is cheaper than this watch.
   　　　= That watch is cheaper than this one.
   　　　= That watch is less expensive than this one.
   中譯：那隻錶比這隻便宜。

捌、以使役動詞合併

1. My mom made me do something.
   I had to wash the dishes.

   _____.
   答案：My mom made me wash the dishes.
   中譯：我媽叫我去洗碗。

2. My dad let me do something.
   I could go to Coco's concert.

   _____.

   答案：My dad let me go to Coco's concert.
   中譯：我爸讓我去聽 Coco 的演唱會。

玖、其他句型之合併

1. Jenny loves dancing.
   Her sister loves dancing, too.（用 so）

   _____.

   答案：Jenny loves dancing, and so does her sister.
   　　　= Jenny loves dancing, and her sister does, too.
   中譯：Jenny 很喜歡跳舞，而她姊妹也一樣。

2. Jessie's boyfriend is very old.
   He can be her father.（用 enough to...）

   _____.

   答案：Jessie's boyfriend is old enough to be her father.
   中譯：Jessie 的男朋友年紀大到可以當她爸爸。

3. Nina washed the dishes after dinner.
   I helped her.

   _____.

   答案：I helped Nina (to) wash the dishes after dinner.
   中譯：吃完晚飯後，我幫 Nina 洗碗。

4. Jane isn't good at singing.

I'm not good at singing.（用 either）

_____.

答案：Jane isn't good at singing, and I'm not, either.

= Jane isn't good at singing, and neither/nor am I.

中譯：Jane不會唱歌，而我也不會。

※ be good at ⟷ be bad/poor at：擅長 ⟷ 不擅長。

5. Tina was hurt in the car accident.

Her friends were hurt in the car accident, too.（用 as well as）

_____.

答案：Tina as well as her friends was hurt in the car accident.

中譯：Tina和她朋友都在車禍中受傷。

※ be 動詞要與主詞 Tina 一致。

6. I could hear a girl.

A girl was crying in the next room.

_____.

答案：I could hear a girl crying in the next room.

中譯：我聽到隔壁房間有女孩子在哭泣。

7. Ben plays computer games.

He spends too much time on the games.

_____.

答案：Ben spends too much time playing computer games.

中譯：Ben 花太多時間玩電腦遊戲。

8. The boss will be here.

He will be here at 10:30.（用 not... until...）

_____.

答案：The boss will not be here until 10:30.

中譯：老闆要到十點半才會來。

3 句子重組

1. Have _____?
   studied / test / you / for / math / the
   答案：Have you studied for the math test?
   中譯：你有準備數學考試嗎？

2. How many _____?
   been / have / times / to / you / America
   答案：How many times have you been to America?
   中譯：你美國去了幾次？

3. What _____?
   you / are / party / going to / the / wear / to
   答案：What are you going to wear to the party?
   中譯：你要穿什麼去參加派對？

4. Would _____?
   mind / the / opening / you / window
   答案：Would you mind opening the window?
   中譯：你介意把窗戶打開嗎？

貳、雙受詞之重組

1. I _____.

   my / best / friend / bought / a / for / watch / cool

   答案：I bought a cool watch for my best friend.

   　　　= I bought my best friend a cool watch.

   中譯：我買一隻酷錶給我最好的朋友。

   ※ 直接受詞：a cool watch；間接受詞：my best friend。

2. My _____.

   Christmas / gave / girlfriend / me / a / card / yesterday

   答案：My girlfriend gave me a Christmas card yesterday.

   　　　= My girlfriend gave a Christmas card to me yesterday.

   中譯：我女朋友昨天給了我一張耶誕卡。

參、方位之重組

1. The bank _____.

   next / post office / is / the / to

   答案：The bank is next to the post office.

   中譯：銀行在郵局隔壁。

2. The supermarket _____.

   the corner / Park Road / of / on / Market Street / is / and

   答案：The supermarket is on the corner of Park Road and Market
   　　　Street.

   中譯：超市在公園路和市場街的轉角。

3. In _____.

is / the / front of / bus stop / hotel / the

答案：In front of the hotel is the bus stop.

= The bus stop is in front of the hotel.

中譯：旅館的前面是公車站牌。

※ 此為倒裝句型，作強調用。

肆、時態之重組

1. I _____.

taking / when / shower / the / was / a / rang / phone

答案：I was taking a shower when the phone rang.

中譯：電話響的時候，我正在洗澡。

2. Call _____.

get / me / as soon / there / as / you

答案：Call me as soon as you get there.

中譯：你一到那裡就打電話給我。

3. I _____.

working / since / have / here / 1995 / been

答案：I have been working here since 1995.

中譯：我從一九九五年開始就在這裡工作。

4. It _____.

since / left / has / time / Taiwan / been / long / you / a

答案：It has been a long time since you left Taiwan.

= It's a long time since you left Taiwan.

中譯：自從你離開台灣，已經過了好長一段時間。

伍、原級、比較級與最高級之重組

1. Julie _____.

   heavy / her / as / brother / as / is

   答案：Julie is as heavy as her brother.

   中譯：Julie 和她兄弟一樣重／胖。

2. Big _____.

   are / small / usually / ones / more / than / books / expensive

   答案：Big books are usually more expensive than small ones.

   中譯：大本書通常比小本書貴。

3. Jenny _____.

   taller / everyone / is / than / else / in / class / her

   答案：Jenny is taller than everyone else in her class.

   中譯：Jenny是她班上最高的學生。

4. Mike _____.

   the / ran / of / three / fastest / the

   答案：Mike ran the fastest of the three.

   中譯：Mike 是三個人當中跑得最快的一個。

陸、驚嘆句之重組

1. What _____!

   good / is / Tom / boy / a

答案：What a good boy Tom is!
　　　= How good a boy Tom is!
中譯：Tom真是個乖小孩！
【句型】**What + a/an + adj + N + S + is**

2. How _____!
a / funny / it / story / is
答案：How funny a story it is!
　　　= How funny the story is!
　　　= What a funny story it is!
　　　= What a funny story!
中譯：這真是個有趣的故事啊！
【句型】**How + adj + a/an + N + S + is**

柒、動名詞、不定詞之重組

1. Learning _____.
write / easy / to / well / is / so / not / English
答案：Learning to write English well is not so easy.
中譯：要把英文寫作學好並不容易。

2. To _____.
office / in/ one / build / an / building / month / is / possible / not
答案：To build an office building in one month is not possible.
中譯：要一個月內蓋一座辦公大樓是不可能的事。

3. It _____.

very / change / is / hard / mind / to / his

答案：It is very hard to change his mind.

中譯：要改變他的心意並不容易。

4. It _____.

necessary / for / study / students / to / hard / is

答案：It is necessary for students to study hard.

＝Students must study hard.

＝Students have to study hard.

中譯：學生必須用功。

捌、名詞子句之重組

1. Nobody _____.

why / Mary / knows / so / got / angry

答案：Nobody knows why Mary got so angry.

中譯：沒有人知道為什麼 Mary 那麼生氣。

2. I _____.

want / know / if / you / to / me / will / help

答案：I want to know if you will help me.

＝ I want to know whether you will help me.

中譯：我要知道你是不是願意幫我的忙。

3. I _____.

that / man / an / believe / Kenny / honest / is

答案：I believe that Kenny is an honest man.
中譯：我相信 Kenny 是個誠實的人。

4. It _____.

is / that / Nina / good / clear / is / girl / a
答案：It is clear that Nina is a good girl.
中譯：很顯然的，Nina 是個好女孩。

5. I _____.

know / where / is / the / don't / museum
答案：I don't know where the museum is.
中譯：我不知道博物館在哪裡。

6. I'll _____.

forget / what / done / never / to / you / me / have
答案：I'll never forget what you have done to me.
中譯：我永遠也忘不了你對我所做的一切。

玖、副詞子句之重組

1. Be _____.

keep / you / get / Japan / to / in touch / sure / to / when
答案：Be sure to keep in touch when you get to Japan.
中譯：到日本的時候，務必保持聯絡。

2. You _____.

should / catch / the / so that / get up / early / you / may / first train
答案：You should get up early so that you may catch the first train.
中譯：你應該早起以便能趕搭第一班火車。

3. If _____.

   study / pass / you / test / hard / will / the / you

   答案：If you study hard, you will pass the test.

   中譯：如果你用功，你就會通過考試。

4. Although _____.

   Cindy / proud / she / beautiful / is / not / is

   答案：Although Cindy is beautiful, she is not proud.

   中譯：雖然 Cindy 人長得漂亮，但她並不驕傲。

拾、形容詞子句之重組

1. Linda _____.

   brothers / for / company / has / who / two / work / a / toy

   答案：Linda has two brothers who work for a toy company.

   中譯：Linda 有兩個在玩具公司上班的兄弟。

2. I _____.

   man / parents / know / both / are / English / whose / teachers / a

   答案：I know a man whose parents are both English teachers.

   中譯：我認識一個男的，他父母都是英文老師。

3. The building _____.

   Cathy / is / where / old / very / lives

   答案：The building where Cathy lives is very old.

   中譯：Cathy住的那棟大樓非常老舊。

4. The park _____.

near / beautiful / very / my / is / which / house / is

答案：The park which is near my house is very beautiful.

中譯：我家附近的那座公園很漂亮。

5. She _____.

the / I / told / is / about / woman / last / time / you / whom

答案：She is the woman about whom I told you last time.

　　　= She is the woman who/whom I told you about last time.

　　　= She is the woman I told you about last time.

　　　（省略關係代名詞 who/whom）

中譯：她就是上次我跟你提的那個女的。

拾壹、其他句型之重組

1. It _____.

twenty / to / took / minutes / get / by / train / there / me

答案：It took me twenty minutes to get there by train.

中譯：搭火車到那裡花了我二十分鐘。

2. I _____.

too / am / study / tired / to / anymore

答案：I am too tired to study anymore.

　　　= I am so tired that I can't study anymore.

　　　= I am too tired to study any more.

　　　= I am too tired to study any longer.

中譯：我太累了沒辦法再唸下去了。

3. I _____.

　　because / didn't / rain / of / out / the / go / heavy

　　答案：I didn't go out because of the heavy rain.

　　中譯：因為雨下得很大，所以我沒有外出。

4. I _____.

　　talk / how / don't / to / him / to / know

　　答案：I don't know how to talk to him.

　　中譯：我不知道怎麼跟他談話。

5. All _____.

　　have / you / do / to / study / is / hard

　　答案：All you have to do is study hard.

　　　　 = All you have to do is to study hard.

　　　　 = All you have to do is studying hard.

　　中譯：你只要努力用功就可以了。

　　※ 第一句最常用。

Notes

第二章 段落寫作

段落寫作，顧名思義，就是寫一段文章。全民英檢初級考試一般會要求學生根據題目的提示（多為看圖說故事形態）寫出大約五十字左右的短文，其評分標準如下：

（1）是否根據試題冊上的圖片發展文章內容？

（2）是否寫出主題句，再依序發展，最後做總結？

（3）是否善用轉折詞（如 first, then, next, finally, besides等）？

（4）是否懂得如何遣詞用字？

（5）是否變化句型？

當然，文法及句型也要力求正確。

1 段落文章的組成要件

（1）引言／主題句：點出整段文章的主題。

（2）主體／本文：根據主題句，發展文章內容。

（3）結論：根據文章內容做總結，須與主題句相呼應。

2 段落文章必殺句型

壹、五大基本句型

S：主詞，V：動詞，C：補語，O：受詞
DO：直接受詞，IO：間接受詞，OC：受詞補語

（1）【句型】S＋V
   ① They are dancing.
      他們正在跳舞。
   ② It rained heavily last night.
      昨晚雨下得很大。

（2）【句型】S＋V＋C
   ① Jenny is a nurse.
      Jenny 是一名護士。
   ② Mimi was very sad yesterday.
      Mimi 昨天很難過。

（3）【句型】S＋V＋O
   ① Jacky hit a homerun last week.
      上週 Jacky 打了一支全壘打。
   ② I hurt my knee yesterday.
      昨天我傷到膝蓋。

（4）【句型】S＋V＋IO＋DO
   ① My mom gave me a comic book.
      我媽給我一本漫畫。
   ② My uncle showed me a picture.
      我叔叔給我看一張照片。

（5）【句型】S＋V＋O＋OC

　① He made me very angry.　他讓我很生氣。

　② We named our dog Lucky.　我們把我們的狗取名叫 Lucky。

※ 其他相關例句，請參考前面的文法重點整理。

貳、四大變化句型

（1）簡單句：（**Simple Sentence**）

即五大基本句型，一個主詞加上一個述詞所構成的句子。

① Lulu didn't prepare for her English test.

Lulu 沒有準備英文考試。

② This is a beautiful park near our school.

這是我們學校附近一座美麗的公園。

（2）複合句：（**Compound Sentence**）

兩個以上的對等子句所構成的句子，其間用對等連接詞（如 **and, but, or**）連接。

① Some are singing, **and** others are chatting at the party.

在派對上，有些人在唱歌，有些人在聊天。

② He is poor, **but** he is happy.

他雖然窮，但過得很快樂。

（3）複句：（**Complex Sentence**）

一個主要子句（獨立子句）加上一個以上的次要子句（從屬子句）所構成的句子，其間用從屬連接詞（如 **because, when** 等）連接。

① She didn't go to school **because** she was sick.

＝ **Because** she was sick, she didn't go to school.

她沒有去上課，因為她生病了。

② **When** he got home, he was wet through.

= He was wet through **when** he got home.

當他回到家的時候，他全身都溼透了。

（4）複合複句：（**Compound-Complex Sentence**）

含次要子句（從屬子句）的兩個對等子句所構成的句子，或兩個以上的主要子句加上一個以上的從屬子句所構成的句子。

① Amy thought that the test was difficult, but Jane didn't think so.

Amy 認為考試很難，但 Jane 不這麼認為。

② Tamshui is a good place, and I will never forget the time I spent there.

淡水是個好地方，而我永遠也忘不了在那裡渡過的時光。

※ 段落寫作須注意變化句型，不要用單一句型從頭寫到尾，以免單調乏味。

3 初級段落寫作之文體介紹

壹、記敘文

【說明】

記敘文就是把一件事情的經過從頭到尾說出來。

《結構》

故事結構有三：① 開頭（主題句），② 本文（故事的主體或發展），③ 結尾（下結論）。

《時態》

記敘文通常採用過去式，來敘述已經發生過的事件。

《觀點》

敘述的觀點主要有二：① 第一人稱（I, we），② 第三人稱（he, she, they）。

以第一人稱的觀點來敘述事件的經過，感覺比較真實而親切，但有時則過於狹隘。而以第三人稱的觀點來敘述事件的發展，則比較靈活，而無須有所保留。考生可依題目來做抉擇，但不論採取何種觀點，只要把握前述評分的幾項原則即可。亦即：

（1）故事／事件內容必須根據試題冊上的圖片發展。

（2）寫出主題句，再依此敘述事情發生的經過，最後作總結。

（3）善用轉折詞或片語（如 first, then, finally, besides 等）。

（4）用字要恰當。

（5）變化句型。

當然，文法、用字及句型要力求正確無誤。

貳、描寫文

【說明】

描寫文就是用文字把看到的景象描述出來，就像畫畫一樣，讓人一目了然，而心有所感。

《結構》

描寫文結構有三：① 開頭（主題句），② 本文（描述景象的相關細節），③ 結尾（下結論）。

《時態》

描寫文通常採用現在式，來敘述作者／考生當下所看到的景象。

《觀點》

以旁觀者清的立場來敘述場景，不要加油添醋或無中生有。當然，最後可以把自己的觀點融入，做為總結。

範例 1

Andy 昨天去士林夜市大吃一頓。請依照圖片寫一篇約 50 字的短文，來敘述他的遭遇。

參考範文

Last night, Andy went to the Shihlin Night Market and tried his favorite kinds of food. First, he ate stinky tofu and pearl milk tea. Next, he had fried chicken and ice. After that, he tried beef noodles and salad. Finally, he tasted some ice cream. When he got home, he felt very sick.

解　析

（1）文章的第一句（主題句）"Last night, Andy went to the Shihlin Night Market and tried his favorite kinds of food." 即點出本篇所要敘述的主題 —— 逛士林夜市。

（2）接下來幾句（本文）便依照主題句發展下來，敘述 Andy 如何大吃一頓："First, he ate stinky tofu and pearl milk tea. Next, he had fried chicken and ice. After that, he tried beef noodles and salad. Finally, he tasted some ice cream."

（3）最後一句（結論）"When he got home, he felt very sick." 點出他亂吃東西所得到的結果。

（4）轉折詞的運用（如 First, Next, After that, Finally）也十分流暢。

（5）時態用過去式 "Last night, Andy went to the Shihlin Night Market and tried his favorite kinds of food. First, he ate stinky tofu and pearl milk tea. Next, he had fried chicken and ice. After that, he tried beef noodles and salad. Finally, he tasted some ice cream. When he got home, he felt very sick." 符合記敘文的時態要求。

（6）句型正確且有變化，例如有用到簡單句（五大句型，如 "Finally, he tasted some ice cream."）、複合句（如 "Last night, Andy went to the Shihlin Night Market and tried his favorite kinds of food."）及複句（如 "When he got home, he felt very sick."），加上轉折詞的穿針引線，使得文章讀來順暢有味。

現在是禮拜天的早上，你走進公園，請根據圖片寫一篇約 50 字的短文，來描述你所看到的景象。

參考範文

It is Sunday morning, and there are a lot of people in the park near my home. Some are dancing, some are talking, and others are playing ball. Besides, a dog is running after a boy, which is very funny. A family are even having a Bar-B-Q under a tree. It is a sunny day, and many people are having a good time in the park.

解 析

（1）文章的第一句（主題句）"It is Sunday morning, and there are a lot of people in the park." 即點出本篇短文所要描寫的是熱鬧的公園。

（2）接下來幾句（本文）便依照主題句發展下來，描寫作者／考生所看到的景象："Some are dancing, some are talking, and others are playing ball. Besides, a dog is running after a boy, which is very funny. A family are even having a Bar-B-Q under a tree."

（3）最後一句（結論）"It is a sunny day, and many people are having a good time in the park." 與主題句前後呼應，點出公園熱鬧的景象。

（4）轉折詞的運用（如 Besides），也非常的順暢。

（5）時態用現在簡單式 "It is Sunday morning, and there are a lot of people in the park near my home." "It is a sunny day, and many people are having a good time in the park." 及現在進行式 "Some are dancing, some are talking, and others are playing ball. Besides, a dog is running after a boy, which is very funny. A family is having a Bar-B-Q under a tree. It is a sunny day, and many people are having a good time in the park." 符合描寫文的時態需求。

（6）句型正確且有變化，例如有用到簡單句（五大句型，如 "A family are having a Bar-B-Q under a tree."）、複合句（如 "It is Sunday morning, and there are a lot of people in the park near my home." "Some are dancing, some are talking, and others are playing ball." "It is a sunny day, and many people are having a good time in the park."）及複句（如 "A boy is running after a dog, which is very funny."），表示有變化。

Notes

第三章 模擬測驗及解答

全民英語能力分級檢定測驗
初級寫作能力測驗模擬試題

試題卷

將答案寫在寫作能力測驗答案紙對應的題號旁，如有拼字、標點、大小寫之錯誤，將予扣分。

第 1～5 題：句子改寫

請依題目之提示，將原句改寫成指定型式，並將改寫的句子完整地寫在答案紙上（包括提示之文字及標點符號）。

1. **The school bus leaves at 7.**
   When _____?

2. **Ken went swimming yesterday.**
   Ken _____tomorrow.

3. **Where is the station?**
   Do you know _____?

4. **I spent one hour getting to the airport.**
   It _____ the airport.

5. **Studying English is a lot of fun.**
   It _____.

第 6～10 題：句子合併

請依題目之提示，將兩句合併成一句，並將合併的句子完整地寫在答案紙上（包括提示之文字及標點符號）。

6. Joe plays video games.
   He wastes too much time on these games.
   _____.

7. Judy is an American student.
   She speaks Chinese very well.（用 who）
   _____.

8. Where is the new English teacher from?
   I don't know.
   _____.

9. Nina asked me a question.
   The question was, "Can you do the job?"
   （用 whether）
   _____.

10. Jack is taller than Ben.
    Ben is taller than James.（用最高級形容詞）
    _____.

請將題目中所有提示字詞整合成一有意義的句子，並將重組的句子完整地寫在答案紙上（包括提示之文字及標點符號）。答案中必須使用所有提示字詞，且不能隨意增加字詞，否則不予計分。

11. What _____?
    you / party / wear / going to / are / to / the

12. My sister _____.
    been / piano / for / has / ten years / playing / the

13. How _____!
    People / are / your / in / family / many / there

14. It's _____.
    three / since / been / you / Taiwan / years / left

15. I _____.
    go / sick / didn't / to / because / was / school / I

第二部分：段落寫作

請依照題目要求，寫一篇約 **50** 字的段落。本部分採整體式評分（**0～5** 級分），再轉換成百分制。評分要點包括重點表達的完整性、文法、用字、拼字、字母大小寫、標點符號。

題目：

Mark 今天考試，但他昨晚卻沒有好好用功，因此考壞了。請根據這些圖片寫一篇約 **50** 字的短文。

Notes

全民英語能力分級檢定測驗
初級寫作能力測驗模擬試題

解答卷

將答案寫在寫作能力測驗答案紙對應的題號旁，如有拼字、標點、大小寫之錯誤，將予扣分。

第 1～5 題：句子改寫

> 請依題目之提示，將原句改寫成指定型式，並將改寫的句子完整地寫在答案紙上（包括提示之文字及標點符號）。

1. The school bus leaves at 7.
   When _____?
   答案：When does the school bus leave?
   中譯：校車幾點開？
   解析：此題考 wh- 問句之現在簡單式：
   　　　Wh-疑問詞 + 助動詞 + S + V原形？

2. Ken went swimming yesterday.
   Ken _____**tomorrow.**
   答案：Ken will go swimming tomorrow.
   　　　= Ken is going to go swimming tomorrow.
   中譯：Ken 明天要去游泳。
   解析：此題考未來簡單式：
   　　　S + will + V原形 + 未來時間
   　　　S + be going to + V原形 + 未來時間

3. Where is the station?
   Do you know _____?
   答案：Do you know where the station is?

中譯：你知道車站在哪裡嗎？

解析：此題考間接問句的用法：

助動詞 + S + V原形 + wh-疑問詞 + S + 普通動詞／Be動詞？

① Do you know where she is?

你知道她人在哪裡嗎？

② Do you know where she lives?

你知道她住在哪裡嗎？

4. I spent one hour getting to the airport.

It _____ the airport.

答案：It took me one hour to get to the airport.

中譯：我花了一個小時才到達機場。

解析：此題考單字 spend（過去式 spent）與 take（過去式 took）的用法：

人 + spent + 時間 + V-ing

It + took + 人 + 時間 + to + V原形

5. Studying English is a lot of fun.

It _____.

答案：It is a lot of fun to study English.

中譯：學英語很有趣。

解析：此題考假／虛主詞與動名詞（V-ing）／不定詞（to + V原形）之互換：

It is + 形容詞／名詞 + to + V原形

= To + V原形 + is + 形容詞／名詞

= V-ing + is + 形容詞／名詞

① It is great to work with him.

= To work with him is great.

= Working with him is great.

跟他共事很棒。

② It is a pleasure to work for him.

    = To work for him is a pleasure.

    = Working for him is a pleasure.

替他工作是件愉快的事。

※ 上面兩個例句亦可寫成：

    ① It is great working with him.

    ② It is a pleasure working for him.

    但初級英檢比較不考此類句型。

第 **6**～**10** 題：句子合併

> 請依題目之提示，將兩句合併成一句，並將合併的句子完整地寫在答
> 案紙上（包括提示之文字及標點符號）。

6. Joe plays video games.

   He wastes too much time on these games.

   _____.

答案：Joe wastes too much time playing video games.

中譯：Joe 浪費太多時間打電動。

解析：此題考單字 waste 的用法：（同 spend 的用法）

    S + waste + 時間 + V-ing

    S + waste + 時間 + on + 名詞

7. Judy is an American student.

   She speaks Chinese very well.（用 **who**）

   _____.

答案：Judy is an American student who speaks Chinese very well.

中譯：Judy 是一個中文講得很棒的美國學生。

解析：此題考形容詞子句的用法：因 Judy 是人，所以關係
代名詞用 who，又因是限定用法，所以 who 前面不
加逗點。（詳見文法重點子句篇，或寫作題型全都錄）

8. Where is the new English teacher from?
I don't know.

_____.

答案：I don't know where the new English teacher is from.

中譯：我不知道新的英文老師是哪裡人。

解析：此題考間接敘述的用法：

S + V + wh-疑問詞 + S + V

① I don't know where John is.

② I don't know where John lives.

9. Nina asked me a question.
The question was, "Can you do the job?"
（用 whether）

_____.

答案：Nina asked me whether I could do the job.

= Nina asked me whether I could do the job or not.

= Nina asked me whether or not I could do the job.

= Nina asked me if I could do the job.

中譯：Nina 問我是否能勝任這項工作。

解析：此題考名詞子句的用法：

S + V + O + whether/if + S + V

10. Jack is taller than Ben.
Ben is taller than James.（用最高級形容詞）

_____.

答案：Jack is the tallest of the three (boys).

中譯：Jack 是三個人當中長得最高的一個。

解析：S + be + the + adj-est/most adj + of the three...

S + be + the + adj-est/most adj + in the/one's class

① Judy is the fattest of the three (girls).

Judy 是三個女孩當中最胖的一個。

② Mark is the most diligent student in his class.

Mark是他班上最勤奮的學生。

※ 兩人作比較用比較級形容詞，而三人以上作比較，則用最高級形容詞。

第 11～15 題：重組

請將題目中所有提示字詞整合成一有意義的句子，並將重組的句子完整地寫在答案紙上（包括提示之文字及標點符號）。答案中必須使用所有提示字詞，且不能隨意增加字詞，否則不予計分。

11. **What** _____?

you / party / wear / going to / are / to / the

答案：What are you going to wear to the party?

中譯：你派對準備穿什麼／你要穿什麼去參加派對？

解析：此題考 wh- 問句之未來式的用法：

Wh-疑問詞 + be + S + going to + V...

※ 做重組題目時，切記遵循一步一步來的原則，同時把握「五大基本句型」，亦即先找主詞，再找動詞，之後依序挑出受詞或補語。當然也要配合相關文法，如時態、子句、疑問句…等。

12. My sister _____.

been / piano / for / has / ten years / playing / the

答案：My sister has been playing the piano for ten years.

中譯：我的姐妹彈鋼琴已經彈了十年。

解析：此題考時態現在完成進行式的用法：

S + have/has + been + V-ing + for + 一段時間

S + have/has + been + V-ing + since + 過去時間

S + have/has + been + V-ing + since + S + V過去式

① I have been studying English for five years.
我唸英文已經唸了五年了。

② I have been studying English since 1999.
我從一九九九年就開始唸英文。

③ I have been studying English since I was ten.
我從十歲就開始唸英文。

13. How _____!

People / are / your / in / family / many / there

答案：How many people are there in your family?

中譯：你家裡有幾個人？

解析：此題考 how many 的用法：

How many + 可數名詞 + are there + in...

How many + 可數名詞 + do/does + S + V原形

① How many students are there in this class?
這個班有幾個學生？

② How many brothers do you have?
你有幾個兄弟？

③ How many baseball cards does he have?
他有幾張棒球卡？

※ How <u>much</u> + 不可數名詞 + <u>is</u> there + in...
How much + 不可數名詞 + do/does + S + V原形

14. It's _____.

three / since / been / you / Taiwan / years / left

答案：It's been three years since you left Taiwan.

中譯：你離開台灣已經三年了。

解析：此題考 since 的用法：

It has been + 一段時間 + since + S + V過去式

It is + 一段時間 + since＋S + V過去式

S + have/has + p.p. + since + S + V過去式

S＋ + have/has + p.p. + since + 過去時間

① It's been a long time since you left us.

你離開我們已有好長一段時間。

② It's two weeks (now) since I wrote to you.

我寫信給你到現在已經兩個星期了。

③ Landy has lived in Japan since her father died.

Landy 自從父親死後就一直住在日本。

④ I have stayed here since March.

我從三月以來就一直待在這裡。

15. I _____.

go / sick / didn't / to / because / was / school / I

答案：I didn't go to school because I was sick.

中譯：我沒有去上學，因為我生病了。

解析：此題考 because 的用法：

S + V + because + S + V

Because + S + V, S + V

I didn't go to the party because I had a cold.

＝ Because I had a cold, I didn't go to the party.

＝ I had a cold, so I didn't go to the party.

我沒有去派對，因為我感冒了。

※ 註：because 和 so 不可並用，即不可以同時出現在一個句子裡。所謂「漢賊不兩立」也。

第二部分：段落寫作

請依照題目要求，寫一篇約 **50** 字的段落。本部分採整體式評分
（**0～5** 級分），再轉換成百分制。評分要點包括重點表達的完整
性、文法、用字、拼字、字母大小寫、標點符號。

題目：
Mark 今天考試，但他昨晚卻沒有好好用功，因此考壞了。
請根據這些圖片寫一篇約 50 字的短文。

參考範文：

　　Mark had a test this morning, but he didn't prepare for it.
Although he is very smart, he is not a good student. Last
night, he didn't study for the test. First he watched TV. Then
he played computer games. In fact, he didn't go to bed until
three o'clock in the morning. That's why he failed today's test.

中譯：

　　Mark 今天早上要考試，可是他並沒有準備。雖然他很聰明，
但是他並不用功。昨天晚上他並沒有準備考試。他先是看電視，
然後玩電腦遊戲。事實上，他到凌晨三點才去睡覺。因此，他今
天考試不及格。

解析：

（1）文章的第一句 "Mark had a test this morning, but he didn't prepare for it." 即點出本篇作文的主題。接下來幾句即依此主題句發展下去，敘述他如何不用功，最後一句「That's why he failed today's test.」做為總結，文章前後呼應，一氣呵成。

（2）轉折詞的運用（如First, Then），亦十分順暢。

（3）時態使用過去式，亦符合記敘文的要求。

（4）句型有用到簡單句（五大句型）（如 "Last night, he didn't study for the test."）、複合句（如 "Mark had a test this morning, but he didn't prepare for it."）及複句（如 "Although he is very smart, he is not a good student."），加上轉折詞運用得當，使得文章讀來順暢有味，而且切合要點。

關鍵字彙庫
Word Bank

A

accident　意外
active　主動的，積極的
afraid　害怕的
age　年齡
air-conditioned　有空調的
almost　幾乎，差不多
along　沿～（的兩側）
America　美國
American　美國人
animal　動物
answer　答案，回答
art　藝術
attend　上（學）
avoid　避免

B

back　返回
baseball　棒球
basketball　籃球
bath　沐浴
beach　海灘
beautiful　漂亮的
because　因為
become　變為，成為
beef　牛肉
believe　相信

bench　長凳
between　在～和～之間
bicycle　腳踏車
bill　帳單
billion　十億
birthday　生日
bite　咬
　（bite, bit, bitten）
block　街區
bookbag　書包
bookstore　書店
bored　感到無聊的
boring　令人感到無聊的
borrow ⟷ lend
　借入（from）⟷ 借出（to）
brand　廠牌
bread　麵包
breakfast　早餐
brother　兄弟
build　建造
bush　矮灌木叢
business　工作；生意；事務
businessman　商人
busy　忙碌的
buy　買

C

cake　蛋糕；餅
call　稱為；打電話；叫

cancer　癌

card　卡片

carefully　仔細地；小心地

catch　接（球）

celebrate　慶祝

change　改變；零錢

cheap　便宜的

children　孩子；兒童

Chinese　中國的

Christmas　耶誕節

church　教堂

class　課；班

classmate　同學

clean　打掃

clearly　清楚地

clerk　店員

clock　鐘

closet　衣櫥

coke　可樂

cold　寒冷的

color　顏色，彩色

comfortable　舒服的

comic book = comics　漫畫書

communication　傳播；通訊

computer　電腦

concentrate　專心，專注

control　控制

convenient　方便的

conversation　會話，對話

cook　煮（飯），做菜

cookie　餅乾

cool　涼爽的

copy　抄寫；影印；一份

corner　（街）角；轉角處

country　國家；鄉下

cousin
　堂（表）兄（弟、姊、妹）

create　創造

criticize　批評

cute　可愛的

D

dance　跳舞

dangerous　危險的

dark　黑暗的

daughter　女兒

dead　死的

decide　決定

decorate　布置

delicious　美味的

dessert　甜點

dialogue　對話

dictionary　字典

diet　飲食
　（go on a diet　在節食）

difference　差別

difficult　困難的

dinner　晚餐

dish　盤子；菜餚

doctor　醫生

dollar　元
doorbell　門鈴
downstairs　下樓
draw　作畫
dress　洋裝
driver　司機
dry　乾的
during　在～期間

E

early　早
east　東方（的）；朝東
easy　容易的
eight　八
either　也不
elementary school　小學
eleven　十一
e-mail　電子郵件
embarrassing　令人難堪的
end　結束
England　英國；英格蘭
English　英語
enjoy　喜歡，享受
enough　足夠的
enter　進入
envelope　信封
Europe　歐洲
ever　曾經（用於問句）
exam = examination　考試

examine　檢查，檢驗
example　例子
exciting　令人興奮的
exercise　運動；作業練習
expensive　昂貴的
experience　經驗

F

factory　工廠
fake　仿冒品，假貨
fall = autumn　秋天
family　家人；家族
famous　有名的
fan　迷；扇子；風扇
fashionable　流行的
father　父親
fault　過錯
favorite　最喜愛的
fifteen　十五
fifty　五十
finally　最後
finger　手指
finish　完成，做完
first　第一
fish　魚
fishing　釣魚
flight　班機
floor　地板
flower　花

follow　遵循
food　食物
foreign　外國的
forget　忘記
fourteen　十四
fourth　第四
free　空閒的
fresh　新鮮的
Friday　星期五
friend　朋友
fries = French fries　炸薯條
fun　樂趣
funny　可笑的，滑稽的
future　未來

G

gain　增加
garbage　垃圾
garden　花園
gentle　溫和的；溫柔的
glasses　眼鏡
grade　分數
graduate　畢業（from）
granddaughter　孫女
grandmother　祖母
grandson　孫子
great　很棒
ground　地面
grownup = adult　大人，成人

guitar　吉他
gym　體育館

H

hair　頭髮
hamburger　漢堡
handsome　英俊的
happen　發生
happy　快樂的
hard　努力地
harm　傷害
hate　討厭
head　頭
health　健康
heavily　猛烈地
heavy　重的
help　幫忙；援助
hike　健行
history　歷史
hold　捧；握
holiday　假日
homework　家庭作業
hope　希望
hospital　醫院
hot spring　溫泉
house　房子；家
housework　家事
hundred　百
hungry　餓（的）

hurry   趕快（up）
hurt   受傷
husband   丈夫

I

idea   主意，想法
ideal   理想的
illegal   違法的
imagine   想像
important   重要的
impossible   不可能的
impressed
　　對…印象深刻的（with/by）
interest   興趣
interesting   有趣的
invention   發明
invite   邀請；招待

J

jacket   夾克
jog   慢跑
　　（jog, jogged, jogging）
join   參加，加入
junior high school   國中

K

keep   保留；飼養
Kenting National Park
　　墾丁國家公園
kilo = kilogram   公斤
kind   種類；親切的
kitchen   廚房

L

language   語言
large   大號的
late   晚，遲
Latin   拉丁文（語）
learn   學習
learner   學習者
leave   留下東西；離開
　　（leave, left, left）
left   左方（的）
leg   腿
lesson   課
letter   信；字母
lick   舔
light   光線；輕的
like（be like）   像；如同
link   連結
little   很少的
live   住

living 活的；生活
living room 客廳
lock 鎖上
loudly 大聲地
low 低
luck 運氣
lucky 幸運的
lunch 午餐

M

machine 機器
married 已婚的
mate 對象；伴侶
math 數學
maybe 也許
medicine 藥
medium 中等的，中間的；
　　五分熟的，半熟的
might 可能
milk 牛奶
million 百萬
minute 分鐘
Miss 小姐
miss 想念；錯過
Mom 媽媽
Monday 星期一
month 月分
mop 拖（地板等）
motorcycle 機車

motorcyclist 機車騎士
mountain 山
move 移動
movie 電影
MRT 捷運
museum 博物館

N

news 新聞，消息
newspaper 報紙
nice 好的；好看的；親切的
noise 噪音
notebook 筆記本
notice 注意到
novel 小說
number 號碼，數字

O

o'clock 點鐘
office 辦公室
often 常常；時常
once 一次
own 自己的；擁有

P

pair   一副，一雙
pants   褲子
parents   雙親
passenger   乘客
PE = physical education   體育
pencil   鉛筆
people   人；人們
perhaps   或許
piano   鋼琴
picture   圖畫
pizza   披薩
place   地方
plane = airplane   飛機
play   打（球）；彈奏
player   球員，選手
please   請
point   要點；分數
police officer   警官，警察
police station   警察局
polite ⟷ impolite
  有禮貌的 ⟷ 不禮貌的
pollution   污染
poor   貧窮的；不好的
popular   流行的
pork   豬肉
poster   海報
practice   練習
prepare   準備；預備（for）

prescription   處方
present   禮物
pretty   漂亮的；十分
preview   預習
price   價錢
problem   問題
produce   產生
proud   自豪的（of）

Q

question   問題
quick   迅速的
quiet   安靜的
quit   戒掉；停止
  （quit, quit, quit）
quite   相當地

R

read   讀
relax   放鬆
remember   記得
report   報導
restaurant   餐館
return   回到
review   複習
rice   米飯
ride   騎；乘

right　　右邊（的）；對的，沒錯

right ⟷ wrong

　　正確的 ⟷ 錯的

road　　（道）路

roller-skate　　溜冰

roof　　屋頂

rule　　規則

S

sad　　難過的，傷心的

safe　　安全的

salad　　沙拉

same　　相同的

Saturday　　星期六

save　　保留；解救

scare　　驚嚇，使恐懼

science　　科學；理化

seafood　　海鮮；海產

season　　季節

seat　　座位；使入座

　　（be seated = sit down）

second　　第二

second-hand = used　　二手的

seldom　　很少；難得

semester = term　　學期

send　　寄發

senior high school　　高中

sentence　　句子

serious　　嚴重的

several　　幾個，數個

shine　　照耀

shoe　　鞋子

shopping　　購物

short　　矮的；短的

shot　　投籃

should　　應該

sick　　生病的

since　　自從

singer　　歌手

sister　　姊妹

size　　尺寸；大小

sky　　天空，天

slowly　　慢慢地

snack　　點心，零食

soccer　　足球

softball　　壘球

software ⟷ hardware

　　軟體 ⟷ 硬體

solve　　解決

sometimes　　有時候

song　　歌曲

soup　　湯

space　　空位

speak　　說

speaker　　講話者

special　　特別的

spell　　拼字

spend　　花費

sport　　運動

spread　　鋪；攤開；散佈

spring	春天	talent	才能
start	開始;出發,動身	talk	講話;說話
station	站;所	tall	高的
stay	留下;待著	tape	錄音帶;膠布
steak	牛排	taxi	計程車
stop	公車(招呼)站	teach	教
strange	奇怪的	teacher	老師
stranger	陌生人	team	隊伍
street	街道	telephone	電話
strict	嚴格的	television	電視
strong	健壯的	terrible	可怕的
student	學生	test	測驗
study	研讀	theater	戲院
stupid	笨的;土土的	these	這些
subject	科目	thin	瘦的
subway	地下鐵	think	想
summer	夏天	third	第三
Sunday	星期日	thirsty	口渴的
Superman	超人	thirteen	十三
supermarket	超級市場	those	那些
Superwoman	女超人	thousand	千
sure	當然;確定的	through	穿過
surprised	驚訝的	Thursday	星期四
sweater	毛衣	ticket	車票;入場券
swim	游泳	tip	秘訣;提示;小費
system	系統	tired	疲倦的
		today	今天
		together	一起
T		tomorrow	明天
		tonight	今夜
		touch	接觸
Taiwan	台灣		

tow　　拖吊

toward　　朝著

towel　　毛巾

town　　小鎮

toy　　玩具

traffic　　交通

train　　火車

tree　　樹

trip　　旅行

try　　試，嘗試

Tuesday　　星期二

turn　　轉（彎、身）

twelve　　十二

twenty-one　　二十一

twice　　二次

twin　　雙胞胎之一

typhoon　　颱風

U

under　　在～下面

underground　　地下的

unhappy　　不愉快的

unusual　　不尋常的

use　　使用

useful　　有用的

V

vacation　　假期

vacuum　　用吸塵器打掃

vacuum cleaner　　吸塵器

vegetable　　蔬菜

vendor　　攤販

video　　錄影帶；影像

village　　村莊

visit　　拜訪，訪問

voice　　聲音，嗓子

volunteer　　自願；志工

W

wait　　等候

waiter　　男服務生

wallet　　錢包，皮夾

warm　　溫暖的

wash　　洗

waste　　浪費

watch　　手錶；看

water　　水

weak　　衰弱的，柔弱的

wear　　穿；戴

weather　　天氣

Wednesday　　星期三

weed　　除草；雜草

week　　星期；週

weekend　　週末

weight　　體重

weigh　　重達…，稱重

welcome　　受歡迎的；歡迎

west　　西方；西邊的；朝西

wet　　潮溼的

whether　　是否

which　　哪一個

wind　　風

wine　　葡萄或其他水果製的酒

winter　　冬天

wish　　祝福

woman　　女人

won　　贏（win 的過去式）

wonder　　想知道，納悶

wonderful　　很棒的；奇妙的

word　　文字

worker　　工人

world　　世界

worried　　煩惱的，發愁的

worse　　較壞的，更壞的

worst　　最壞的

write　　寫

wrong　　錯的

Z

zebra　　斑馬

zero　　零

zoo　　動物園

Y

yellow　　黃色

younger　　年幼的

yo-yo　　溜溜球

重要片語群

A

a basketball game　一場籃球賽
a big dinner　一頓豐盛的晚餐
a class in a cram school
　補習班的課
a glass of　一杯
a good pair of shoes
　一雙好的鞋子
a little　一點點
a long day of work
　一整天的工作
a long time　很久一段時間
a lot of　許多
a science class　理化課
a week after Christmas
　聖誕節過後一星期
after a while　過了一會兒
after all　終究，畢竟
after class　下課後
after dinner　晚餐後
after school　放學後
after the baseball game
　棒球賽之後
after work　下班後
again and again　再三地
all morning　整個早上
all the time = at all times
　始終，一直
an English class　一節英文課

answer to...　～的答案
Anything else?　還要別的嗎？
Anything to drink?
　要喝什麼嗎？
as soon as　一～就～
ask questions　問問題
ask + 人 + for + 物
　向某人要求某物
at a time　一次，同時
at about four o'clock　大約四點
at bedtime　在就寢時間
at first　起先，最初
at home　在家
at school　在學校；在上課
at the beach　在海邊
at the door　在門口
at the right place　在適當的地點
at the right time　在適當的時機

B

baseball card　棒球卡
basketball card　籃球卡
be active in　主動～
be afraid of　害怕
be badly hurt　受傷嚴重
be embarrassed about
　對～感到尷尬
be fond of　喜歡，愛好

257

be good at ←→ be bad/poor at
精通 ←→ 不善於
be happy for　為～而高興
be interested in　對～感興趣
be made in + 地方　在某地製造
be nice to　對～親切
be proud of　以～為榮
be ready to + 原形動詞
準備好要～
be surprised at　對～驚訝
be worried about　對～擔心
become busier　變得較忙
before class　上課前
best wishes　由衷的祝福
between... and...　在～和～之間
between classes　下課時間
bump into = run into = run across
撞上；偶遇
buy + 物 + for + 人
買某物給某人
by bus/subway
搭乘公車／地下鐵
by the way　順便一提

C

carefully ←→ carelessly
仔細地；小心地 ←→ 疏忽地
catch a baseball　接到棒球
cell phone　手機

Chinese New Year　農曆春節
Chinese New Year's Eve
農曆除夕
Christmas Eve　聖誕夜，平安夜
come/be from　來自於～
come after...　在～之後來
come back for the New Year
回來過年
Come on in.　進來。
come to　來到
come with...　和～一起來
concentrate on　專心於
country life　鄉下生活
cram school　補習學校，補習班
credit card　信用卡

D

dead languages　死的語言
department store　百貨公司
die of　因疾病或飢餓而死
dining room　飯廳
do well on... test　～考試考得好
do you good　對你有益處

E

eat a lot　吃得多
excuse me　對不起；請問

F

fall asleep　　睡著

far away from　　遠離

for a long time　　好久

for a short while　　短時間

for a while　　暫時

for example = for instance
　　例如

for more than ten years
　　超過十年

for your own health
　　為了你自己的健康

G

get home　　到家

get on/off　　上／下車

get out of　　從～出來

get to　　到達

get up early　　早起床

give an example　　舉例

give up + V-ing　　放棄做～

give + 物 + to + 人
　　把某物給某人

go along　　沿著～走

go back to...　　返回～

go dancing　　去跳舞

go home together　　一起回家

go on a diet　　進行節食

go out　　外出

go shopping　　去購物

go swimming　　去游泳

go to a baseball game
　　去看場棒球比賽

go to a cram school　　上補習班

go to a junior high school in + 某地
　　去上～的一所國中

go to a math class　　上數學課

go to a movie　　去看電影

go to ball games　　去看球賽

go to bed　　去睡覺

go to church　　上教堂做禮拜

go to school　　去上學

go to the same class　　上同一班級

good luck　　祝好運

graduate from　　從～畢業

grow and change with time
　　隨著時間成長與演變

grow up　　長大，成長

H

have a bad day
　　過不愉快的一天；倒楣

have a big dinner　　吃大餐

have a coke　　喝杯可樂

have a good time　　玩得開心

have a party　　舉行派對

have a test　　舉行測驗

have dinner　　吃晚餐

have ever been to　　曾到過

have milk　　喝牛奶

have no interest in
　　對～不感興趣

have the wrong number
　　打錯電話

help + 人 + with + 事
　　幫某人做～

Here you are.
　　你要的東西在這裡。

How are you doing?　　你好嗎?

how many + 複數可數名詞
　　多少

how much + 不可數名詞　　多少

how often　　多久一次

how old　　幾歲

how tall　　多高

How've you been?
　　你近來好嗎?

I

I see.　　我明白了。

in bed　　在睡覺

in class　　上課中

in different classes
　　在不同的班級

in fact　　事實上

in front of　　在～的前面

in life　　一生中

in one's third year of junior high
　　某人國中三年級

in the accident　　在意外事故中

in the afternoon　　在下午

in the dialogue　　在對話中

in the future　　在未來

in the kitchen　　在廚房裡

in the mountains　　在山上

in the newspaper　　報紙上

in the past ←→ in the future
　　在過去 ←→ 在未來

in the same class　　在同一班

in the supermarket　　在超市裡

in the tree　　在樹上

in the U.S.　　在美國

in the water　　在水中

in the world = on earth
　　在世界上;究竟

in traffic jams　　在交通阻塞中

invite + 人 + to dinner
　　招待某人吃晚餐

It's no use.　　一點用也沒有。

J

join　　參加,加入

jump out of bed　　跳下床

不規則動詞變化表

原形/現在式	過去式	過去分詞	中文字義
be (am/is/are)	was/were	been	是;成為;(存)在
become	became	become	變成;變得
begin	began	begun	開始
beat	beat	beaten	打;擊;打敗
bite	bit	bitten	咬
blow	blew	blown	吹
break	broke	broken	打破;打斷
bring	brought	brought	帶來
build	built	built	建造
burn	burnt/burned	burnt/burned	燒;燒掉;燒焦
buy	bought	bought	購買
catch	caught	caught	抓(到);搭(車);接(住)
choose	chose	chosen	選擇
come	came	come	來(到)
cost	cost	cost	花費
cut	cut	cut	切,砍;割傷
dig	dug	dug	挖(出)
do	did	done	做
draw	drew	drawn	畫;拉;提領
dream	dreamt/dreamed	dreamt/dreamed	作夢;夢見
drink	drank	drunk	喝
drive	drove	driven	開車;駕駛
eat	ate	eaten	吃
fall	fell	fallen	落下;跌倒
feed	fed	fed	餵
feel	felt	felt	感覺;覺得;摸起來(後接形容詞)
fight	fought	fought	打架;吵架
find	found	found	尋找;找到
fly	flew	flown	飛
forget	forgot	forgot/forgotten	忘記
forgive	forgave	forgiven	原諒

原形/現在式	過去式	過去分詞	中文字義
get	got	got/gotten	得到；取得；變得
give	gave	given	給
go	went	gone	去；開始；變得
grow	grew	grown	成長；變得
have	had	had	有；吃；喝；使
hear	heard	heard	聽（到）
hide	hid	hidden	躲；藏
hit	hit	hit	打；擊中
hold	held	held	握；抓；拿；保持
hurt	hurt	hurt	傷害；受傷
keep	kept	kept	保持
know	knew	known	知道；了解；認識
lead	led	led	領導；引導；過著
learn	learnt/learned	learnt/learned	學習；知道；得知
leave	left	left	離開；留給；使得
lend	lent	lent	借出；借給（～to）
let	let	let	讓
lose	lost	lost	遺失；迷失；輸掉
make	made	made	做；製做；使
mean	meant	meant	意為；有意
meet	met	met	遇見；會面
mistake	mistook	mistaken	誤解；誤認為
oversleep	overslept	overslept	睡過頭
pay	paid	paid	付；付出
prove	proved	proven	證明
put	put	put	放；置於
quit	quit/quitted	quit/quitted	戒掉；辭職；退出；放棄
read	read	read	讀；唸
ride	rode	ridden	騎；乘
ring	rang	rung	鈴響；按鈴；打電話
rise	rose	risen	上升；起立
run	ran	run	跑；經營

原形/現在式	過去式	過去分詞	中文字義
say	said	said	說
see	saw	seen	看；看見；了解
sell	sold	sold	賣；銷售
send	sent	sent	發送；郵寄；派遣
set	set	set	放；置；設定
shake	shook	shaken	搖動；握（手）
shine	shone/shined	shone/shined	照耀／擦亮
show	showed	shown/showed	顯示；出示；放映
shut	shut	shut	關上；合上
sing	sang	sung	唱歌
sink	sank/sunk	sunk/sunken	沉；使下沉
sit	sat	sat	坐下
sleep	slept	slept	睡覺
smell	smelt/smelled	smelt/smelled	聞；聞起來（後接形容詞）
speak	spoke	spoken	說，講
spend	spent	spent	花費；花時間
stand	stood	stood	站立；忍受
steal	stole	stolen	偷竊
strike	struck	struck/striken	打，擊
sweep	swept	swept	打掃；掃除
swim	swam	swum	游泳
take	took	taken	拿；帶；乘坐；花時間
teach	taught	taught	教書；教導
tear	tore	torn	撕；撕開
tell	told	told	告訴；辨別（~from）
think	thought	thought	想；考慮；認為
throw	threw	thrown	丟，投，擲
understand	understood	understood	了解
wake	woke/waked	waken/waked	醒來
wear	wore	worn	穿；戴
win	won	won	贏；賺取
write	wrote	written	寫

國家圖書館出版品預行編目資料

全民英檢初級保證班：閱讀與寫作／初碧
華著. -- 二版. -- 臺北市：書泉出版
社，2024.05
面；　公分
ISBN 978-986-451-375-8(平裝)

1.英語 2.讀本 3.寫作法

805.1892　　　　　　113004801

3AS1

全民英檢初級保證班：
閱讀與寫作

作　　者 ─ 初碧華(452)

發 行 人 ─ 楊榮川

總 經 理 ─ 楊士清

總 編 輯 ─ 楊秀麗

副總編輯 ─ 黃惠娟

責任編輯 ─ 魯曉玟

美術編輯 ─ 米栗設計工作室

插　　畫 ─ 林采彤

封面設計 ─ 鄭依依

出 版 者 ─ 書泉出版社

地　　址：106台北市大安區和平東路二段339號4樓

電　　話：(02)2705-5066　傳　真：(02)2706-6100

網　　址：https://www.wunan.com.tw

電子郵件：shuchuan@shuchuan.com.tw

劃撥帳號：01303853

戶　　名：書泉出版社

總 經 銷：貿騰發賣股份有限公司

電　　話：(02)8227-5988　傳　真：(02)8227-5989

網　　址：http://www.namode.com

法律顧問　林勝安律師

出版日期　2005年11月初版一刷（共十刷）

　　　　　2024年 5 月二版一刷

定　　價　新臺幣350元